UNEXPECTED

HEARTS ON DISPLAY, BOOK TWO

KIMBERLY KEAGAN

Ventana
Publishing

To my son, who has a heart of gold, keeps me laughing, and knows more trivia than one person should.

Hearts on Display

Charles Walraven
(b. 1833)
Co-Founder, Denwall
Department Stores
m. **Laura Shaw**
(b. 1840)

·············· **Robert "Bert"** (b. 1865)

·············· **William "Will"** (b. 1867)
Perfect
BOOK ONE
featuring
Ivy King (b. 1871)
Daughter of Richard King (d. 1893)
Daughter of Rosina Abbott (d. 1893)
Granddaughter of **Jemima King** (b. 1825)
Niece of **Zella Abbott Capp** (b. 1863)

·············· **Edward "Ned"** (b. 1876)

·············· **Caroline "Caro"** (b. 1879)

James Dennison
(b. 1843)
Co-Founder, Denwall
Department Stores
m. Sarah Fenwicke
(b. 1843 d. 1878)
m. **Myra Kuntz**
(b. 1845)

·············· **Max** (b. 1867)

·············· **Helena "Lena"** (b. 1869)

·············· **Louise "Lou"** (b. 1871)

·············· **Beatrice "Bea"** (b. 1876)

·············· **Alexandra "Alix"** (b. 1878)

ONE

Monday, November 11, 1895
Philadelphia, Pennsylvania

If you'd asked him three months ago, getting punched in the ribs wouldn't have been high on Robert Walraven's list of enjoyable early-morning activities. But that was before he woke up in a New York hospital after being mugged in Madison Square Park.

Bert adjusted the tape on his boxing gloves, tugging it tighter than necessary. The rhythmic thud of fists meeting leather filled the upscale athletic club, mingling with the scent of sweat and expensive shaving balm. An exclusive place, gentlemen came to this club to test themselves without the grime of Philadelphia's rougher fighting pits.

He exhaled slowly, rolling his shoulders as he stepped into the ring. His opponent, a wiry man with quick hands, lifted his gloves in silent acknowledgment. Bert mirrored the motion, his muscles humming with restless energy. Rowing, his sport of choice in college, required physical power and strength. Even now, he could feel the tension of the water through an oar, but boxing demanded a different kind of strength—both mental and physical. It demanded complete control.

So that he'd never be caught unaware again.

The bell rang, and Bert moved instinctively, circling left. His sparring partner came in faster than expected, throwing a sharp jab that grazed his temple. He absorbed it, steadied himself. He had always been an athlete, but finesse in the ring wasn't the same as endurance in a boat. His footwork and timing needed more work. Still, he adjusted, countering with a well-placed right that knocked the man off balance.

"What exactly are you doing, Bert?" A familiar voice cut through the clamor of the gym.

Bert startled, taking a hit to the ribs as his focus slipped. He gritted his teeth, stepping back. His sparring partner, recognizing the distraction, backed off with a knowing smirk. Bert turned and squinted toward the source of the voice.

Will stood just inside the doorway, arms crossed, wearing the unimpressed look of a brother catching his oldest sibling in the act of something questionable.

"What are you doing here?" Bert swiped at the sweat running down his forehead as Will stepped closer. "Shouldn't you be getting your beauty sleep before we head to New York for your engagement dinner?" He narrowed his eyes. "And how did you know where to find me?"

"If you remember, there's a board meeting this morning. When I stopped by your place just now, your staff told me where you were."

"Remind me to fire my housekeeper," Bert grumbled. Truth be told, he'd never fire the talkative woman. She kept his personal life in manageable order.

He blew out a breath, grabbed a towel, and picked up his spectacles from the corner of the ring. "You shouldn't be here."

Will lifted an eyebrow. "That's my line."

Bert hopped down from the ring, ignoring the stiffness in his ribs and Will's perceptive gaze.

"How long have you been sneaking in here?"

"I'm not sneaking." Bert wiped his face with the towel.

"Oh? Then why haven't you mentioned it?"

"Because it's no one's business but mine."

Will ran a hand through his hair. "Is this about Madison Square Park?"

"I don't want to talk about that."

"So instead of talking, you come *here*?" Will stepped closer. "What exactly is this supposed to do? Prove that next time someone comes up behind you unawares, you'll be ready?"

Bert clenched his jaw. "You weren't the one lying on the ground, Will." The words came out colder than he intended, but he didn't want to apologize. "I should have been able to stop him. Instead, I woke up in a hospital."

"You were ambushed!"

"That's an excuse. One I don't intend to rely on again."

"Fine. You want to learn to fight? Learn. But don't pretend it's going to undo what happened." Will rubbed his temple as if fighting off a headache. "And for heaven's sake, if you're going to do something that could cause bodily harm, at least tell someone."

"So I can be lectured? No thanks."

Will didn't push further. Instead, he glanced around the club, the sharp clang of weights and the steady drum of sparring filling the silence between them. "Father would hate this."

"That's half the appeal."

"Just ... be careful, all right? You have nothing to prove."

Bert didn't answer right away. Because maybe he needed to prove something to himself. He clapped Will on the shoulder, signaling that the conversation was over.

Will shook his head in defeat. "Well, get dressed and I'll wait for you. We'll go to the office together."

Inside the locker room, Bert gingerly sat on a bench and pulled off his sweaty shirt. The ache in his ribs reminded him he wasn't used to taking punches. A hot shower beckoned him, and although Will was waiting, he wouldn't skip it. Partly to be annoying, and partly because he was in no hurry to continue discussing his new hobby.

The low hum of voices and the clatter of oak lockers opening and closing echoed through the tiled room as he made his way to the showers. Steam clouded the air, curling against the high windows.

He turned the spigot, waited for the rush of hot water, and stepped under. Heat poured over him, loosening his tight muscles. His mind drifted to Will's upcoming engagement dinner. As the eldest brother and best man, Bert would be front and center, of course. It was his duty. The whole family would travel to Manhattan, where Ivy lived and where Will would manage the family's newest Denwall Department Store.

Despite having no interest in marriage himself, Bert didn't scorn Will's upcoming nuptials. In fact, he liked Ivy King and thought her perfect for Will. It didn't hurt that she was a bookseller and an expert in rare books. Ivy's aunt Zella had laughingly told him once that he had more in common with Ivy than Will did.

Zella Capp. What an enigma. Only two years older than he, the bold and daring woman was outgoing to a fault. She navigated social situations with ease, even those involving New York's Four Hundred, the crème de la crème of society, despite growing up on a farm in Ohio.

Bert, on the other hand, preferred books to people, numbers that added up in tidy columns, and solitude over small talk. Where he faded into the woodwork, Zella lit up every room she entered.

And when they were together? She drove him absolutely crazy.

No, he didn't know what to make of the widow Capp, and he didn't like that she made him think about things he preferred to ignore. Like her knowing gray eyes. Or how she filled out a gown.

One thing was for certain, having Zella in the Walraven fold, even as a relative through her niece's marriage, would bring a whole new dynamic to family gatherings.

<hr />

Manhattan, New York

Zella Capp set down her lukewarm tea, forcing a smile she hoped passed for delight. On the eve of her niece's engagement dinner, she felt more mourner than aunt of the bride-to-be.

Across the parlor, Ivy sat on the rug beside the fireplace in the apartment above the Kings' bookshop, her hand resting on the broad head of her Saint Bernard, Dickens. The fire's glow cast flickers of light on the walls, and it's crackle mingled with the soft clack of Jemima's knitting needles. The older woman's pale blue eyes rested on her granddaughter, probably worried about Ivy's quiet mood.

So much must be going through Ivy's head, not the least of which were the managing of the bookshop and the coming changes marriage would bring.

Marriage.

Zella shuddered despite the warmth of the fire. Many considered it a woman's highest calling. To Zella, it seemed as constricting as a corset—tight, uncomfortable, and designed more for a man's benefit than a woman's comfort.

It wasn't that she disapproved. Zella couldn't have chosen

a better husband for Ivy than the heir to Denwall Department Stores.

The ache in Zella's chest had nothing to do with Will Walraven and everything to do with change. Selfish, perhaps, but real. Once Ivy became a wife, and likely a mother, there would be less time for spinster aunts.

At thirty-two, Zella was hardly elderly. But watching Ivy—eight years her junior and on the cusp of a new life—she felt practically fossilized.

Her solitary life had been a choice, to be sure. One she'd made with resolve and no regrets. Still, with Ivy's parents long gone, her niece was Zella's only living blood relative. She had Jemima, of course, dear as kin, but Jemima was well into her seventies. And while Zella knew a great many people, few truly knew her. Once Ivy married, Zella feared she'd be left behind watching life hurry on without her.

Ivy sighed, and Dickens, ever attuned, lowered his chin to her lap and whined.

"Are you all right, dear?" Jemima's brow furrowed in concern.

"Sorry for being so quiet, Gran. I'm just nervous."

"Understandable," Jemima said gently. "But nerves are nothing to fret over. All brides have them." She reached over and patted Ivy's shoulder.

"It's not marrying Will that worries me. I love him, and I know he loves me." Ivy stroked Dickens's head in slow, soothing circles until his eyes slid closed. "It's the dinner tomorrow night. I wish we could simply have it here at home."

Zella chuckled. "How would we fit all eleven guests at your kitchen table, pet? Delmonico's is perfect. Trust me when I say you'll adore it."

"Oh, I'm sure it's lovely. I've heard wonderful things, and we'll have a private room." Ivy picked at her skirt hem.

"You'll look beautiful," Jemima said with a nod. "That cornflower blue dress brings out your eyes."

"And I'll sweep your hair into a style that would make a Gibson Girl jealous." Zella's years as a wealthy lady's companion had left her with a few useful tricks, especially when it came to dressing for elegant affairs.

Ivy smiled and lifted the hem of her skirt just enough to show her new shoes. "At least my shoes aren't hideous."

Crafted from supple high-grade leather, the pair—one shoe subtly elevated to compensate for her shorter leg—had been made by the Denwall cobbler at Will's request. Fashion and function, married to perfection.

Zella admired the quiet dignity with which Ivy bore her challenge. Despite her affliction, she was one of the most graceful women Zella had ever known. Beautiful inside and out. With Will's attention and devotion, she'd blossomed over the last three months. "Will's jaw is going to hit the floor when he sees you."

"Thank you, both. I'm sure it will all be fine."

Zella tilted her head. "Do I hear a *but* in there?"

Ivy hesitated. "Will's father doesn't exactly make me feel welcome."

"He's a crusty old goat," Zella muttered.

"Zella!" Jemima half-scolded, half-laughed, then waved a hand. "Don't give Charles Walraven a second thought, Ivy. Will's love is what matters." Her voice dropped to a whisper. "And if Mrs. Walraven catches her husband being anything less than kind, she'll clobber him."

Zella caught Ivy's eye, and both fought not to giggle.

"Yes, Gran," Ivy said with a straight face. "Will says his mother can be a force to behold."

"And you get along famously with his brother Robert," Jemima added.

"Bert," Ivy corrected gently. "He would like us to call him

Bert. And yes, we have a lot in common. He loves rare books almost as much as I do."

Zella suppressed a sigh. To each their own. She'd rather experience the world than bury her nose in a musty old volume like Bert tended to do. What a stick-in-the-mud.

"How's he doing?" Jemima asked, her voice dropping. "Poor man. Imagine being attacked in Madison Square Park in broad daylight."

"He's glad to be back in Philadelphia, I think. Will says he's fully recovered, thank the Lord."

"After what he's been through, it's a blessing he's back to normal," Jemima added.

It had been a frightening four days, especially for Will, who hadn't left his brother's side at the hospital. Hopefully, Bert was indeed better. No one deserved to be attacked.

Jemima returned to her knitting, and Dickens let out a long, contented sigh. The fire crackled softly as Zella's gaze drifted toward the window. Below, the city hummed with streetcars trundling past, faint voices echoing from the avenue.

For a moment, the conversation faded, each woman lost in her own thoughts.

Zella wrapped her arms around her middle and stared at the world outside the cozy parlor. Perhaps it wasn't only Ivy stepping into something new that left her hollow, but the still-ness of her own life.

She'd chosen solitude years ago and defended it ever since. But lately, it felt more like stagnation than freedom. Maybe it was time for something different. A trip, perhaps. She could pitch a series of feature-length articles for *Harper's Bazaar* from Paris. Or from Vienna.

Something new. Somewhere different.

Two

The next evening
Manhattan

The hansom cab drew up to the curved corner of Delmonico's, where golden lamplight spilled across the damp cobbles. Zella peered out the carriage window, her face tipped to take in the dignified brick façade and marble columns that were just as grand as she remembered, though perhaps a touch more theatrical in the evening fog. Well-dressed patrons bustled beneath the striped awning.

She adjusted her gloves as the footman opened the carriage door. Jemima, still agile at an advanced age, descended first, followed by Ivy. When all three of them were safely on the sidewalk, Zella led them the short distance to the restaurant's front door.

Inside, she inhaled the scent of polished wood, hot-house flowers, and fine perfume as they were guided up the carpeted staircase, each step muffled by thick velvet runners. The crisply dressed maître d' opened a door to a private dining room where guests stood chatting in small clusters. Behind them stretched a dining table, each place already set with shining silver and etched crystal.

At Ivy's request, the affair was small, just the Walraven family, Denwall's co-founder James Dennison, and his wife Myra.

Conversation in the private dining room hushed when the new arrivals crossed the threshold. Thankfully, Zella recognized most of the guests from the grand opening of Denwall's New York store, which had taken place several weeks prior.

Just a few blocks from the Kings' beloved bookshop, the grand emporium had caused quite a stir in the neighborhood and in Ivy's quiet life. But without Denwall, she never would have met Will, who'd been sent from Philadelphia, along with his brother Bert, to get the new store up and running.

Zella didn't despise department stores like many did. As someone who made a living writing about women's fashion, as well as home décor, she understood the many benefits the large stores offered.

In fact, she greatly admired Charles Walraven and James Dennison, who had started Denwall Department Stores with nothing but a small loan and an idea of how to serve customers better. Now, the enterprise had some of the largest emporiums in the country.

Standing by the fireplace with his parents, Will turned and smiled at Ivy like she'd strung up the stars herself. "You look stunning," he told her when he arrived at her side. He lifted her gloved hand and placed a kiss on her knuckles. "Mrs. King, Mrs. Capp, welcome." He slipped Ivy's hand through the crook of his arm and guided her toward his parents.

Chatter soon filled the room once more. Will's maternal grandmother, Mrs. Shaw, engaged Jemima in conversation about the wedding plans, leaving Zella to glance around the room for someone to talk to. Bert was conspicuously absent, so she couldn't engage in witty banter with him, yet she was certain he'd arrived on the train from Philadelphia that morning with everyone else.

Myra Dennison beckoned Zella to join her by the fireplace. She wore a shimmering gown that exuded wealth and privilege, yet her smile was genuine. She, of all people, knew what it was like to be an outsider in this group. From what Ivy had told her, James had married Myra many years after losing his children's mother.

"Mrs. Capp," she said warmly, taking Zella's hand. "How lovely to see you. Ivy looks exquisite, doesn't she? And calm, considering. Most women I know would be pale and trembling."

"Ivy's nerves are made of stronger stuff," Zella said.

"I'm sure her parents would be very proud of her, what with running the bookshop and marrying for love."

Zella's throat tightened. No young woman should have to marry without her parents at her side, and no mother should outlive her son, as Jemima had.

Ivy and Jemima weren't the only ones who felt the pain of Rosina and Richard's deaths in a train accident two years before. The familiar ache at the loss of her sister washed over Zella. So many times since that fateful day, she wished she'd had the courage to drop her life in Chicago and move to New York earlier. Three years getting reacquainted with her sister hadn't been nearly long enough.

But that was water under the bridge now. She'd made her choices in life years ago, and her primary focus had been her career as a lady correspondent. Still was.

Myra placed a gloved hand on Zella's arm. "I'm so sorry, dear. I didn't mean to bring up something so obviously painful."

"No, it's fine. You did nothing wrong." Zella patted Myra's hand and attempted a smile. "You're absolutely correct.

Ivy's parents would have been very proud of her. And Will is perfect for her."

"Yes, William is a dear young man. He—" Myra's voice faltered, and her lips turned up. "Well, there's Robert finally. That young man doesn't know the meaning of punctuality."

Zella flicked her gaze to the doorway as Bert stepped into the room, rain dripping from his hair, his tie slightly askew. Behind wire-rimmed spectacles, his hazel eyes scanned the room with a weariness that sparked Zella's curiosity. She wondered if his tardiness was due to Denwall business or something else entirely.

When his perusal touched on her and Myra, Myra gave him a small wave.

He offered a half-smile and made his way toward them, his steps unhurried. On the way, he pecked his grandmother on the cheek and moved to Ivy to give her a quick one-armed hug. When he reached Myra's side, she wagged a gloved finger at him. "Your father's bound to give you a lecture for being late."

Zella had had enough encounters with the eldest Walraven offspring to know that he marched to the beat of a different drum than those around him, much like herself.

"Yes, I'm sure you're correct about that," he said, shoving his hands into the pockets of his rumpled suit.

"What kept you? Were you buried in Denwall financial reports or some musty old book?" Zella teased him, knowing he wouldn't take offense. In the short time she'd known him, she'd discovered that poking the oldest Walraven son was quite enjoyable.

"Financial reports. Our accounting manager has no sense of accuracy," Bert replied dryly. He tipped his head at Myra. "You look well, Mrs. Dennison."

"Oh, pish, young man. You know we don't stand on formalities."

The maître d' reappeared in the doorway. "Dinner is served."

Footmen pulled out chairs with practiced grace.

Standing at the head of the table, Charles commandeered the seating arrangements, gesturing to Jemima to sit beside his wife while Ivy slipped into the place beside Will.

"Mrs. Capp," Charles said in an imperious tone, "please sit next to Robert."

Zella returned the stiff courtesy with a smile and a nod that tread the polite line between gracious and amused.

"How fortunate for me to sit beside such charming company." Bert pulled out Zella's chair.

Fairly certain he found her chatter annoying, she nearly laughed at his compliment. He slid into the seat on her right, beside his formidable grandmother, who immediately began a whispered scolding.

"Yes, Grandmother," he said patiently. "You're absolutely correct. It is very rude of me to be late."

Apparently satisfied, his grandmother shifted her attention to the waiter, who placed a chilled plate of oysters before her.

"None for me, thank you," Bert said as he waved the server away.

Zella leaned in. "It's a shame you can't enjoy shellfish."

"Not unless you want to see me turn blue." He gave her a self-deprecating smile and a shrug.

Not for the first time, Zella noted the man had a smile that could knock the breath out of a woman.

Delmonico's service was impressive, of course—gleaming chandeliers, the ring of silver against porcelain, and waiters moving with the precision of a well-oiled machine.

Not so long ago, Zella had dined in Parisian salons and Venetian palazzos. The extravagance didn't awe her. Yet this wasn't her world. Not really.

She took a sip of champagne and glanced surreptitiously around the table. The Walravens wore wealth like old money, though they were relatively new to the social elite. Confident, not ostentatious.

Charles and Laura Walraven, seated at the head of the table, were the picture of a well-matched, long-standing marriage. The son of a middle-class bank manager, Charles was dignified, a man who had built an empire with steady hands and a shrewd mind. Laura, with her poised elegance, had clearly ensured that Denwall's success extended beyond business into the social realm. Zella could admire the power coupled with restraint.

The Walraven children all had their mother's chestnut hair and hazel eyes and seemed well adjusted. Will looked at Ivy the way a man should—with admiration, even a little in awe. Ned and Caroline, the youngest, brimmed with youthful energy, but not obnoxiously so. Caroline's watchful eyes hinted at intelligence beyond her years. That kind of perceptiveness in a girl so young was interesting.

Laura's mother, Mrs. Shaw, was a merchant's widow who lived in Boston. From what Ivy said, she refused to budge from the house she and her husband had shared for sixty years. The light in her eyes said she was still as sharp as a tack. During the dessert course, those knowing eyes fixed on Zella like a jeweler inspecting a stone. "I understand you spent time abroad, Mrs. Capp," she said, leaning around Bert.

"Almost four years, on and off."

"How could you afford such a luxury?"

Like many people in their advanced age, Mrs. Shaw had no compunction about asking pointed questions.

Bert groaned. "Grandmother ..."

"It's all right," Zella whispered for his ears alone. In a louder voice, she said, "I was a widow's companion for Florence Ashford of Chicago. She loved to travel and, fortunately for me, I was introduced to places all over the world that I most likely would never have seen otherwise."

"Hmph. And did that broaden your horizons?"

Zella's lips twitched. "It certainly expanded my shoe collection. And my tolerance for endless museum tours."

Bert chuckled, but Mrs. Shaw only narrowed her eyes, clearly filing the information away in her mind.

Zella returned her attention to her plum pudding, but not before catching Caroline's smile of encouragement across the table.

As the evening wound down, the lively hum of conversation softened, and Delmonico's waiters discreetly cleared the last remnants of dinner. Charles declared it had been a long day and he was tired, so everyone filed out of the private dining room and took the stairs down to the lobby.

Zella started to ask a footman to secure a hansom cab when James held up a hand. "Allow us to take you home, Mrs. Capp. I believe Will is going to escort Ivy and Mrs. King to their bookshop, and I understand that our carriage will be going past your apartment."

That made perfect sense. "That's very kind. Thank you."

Soon, they were nestled in the plush Dennison carriage, with James and Myra on one side of the vehicle and Zella on the other.

After polite pleasantries about the weather, their impending return to Philadelphia the next day, and the state of Manhattan's roads, James cleared his throat. "There are rumors that the leading fashion houses of Europe have granted an exclusive preview of next season's styles to a syndicate of American fashion houses. We understand that the group has also received permission to present these new fashions to their American customers when the European houses launch their own reveals in Europe."

An interesting turn in the conversation.

Zella studied James's unreadable face. He'd make a good poker player. "I've heard about it. I understand the syndicate plans to offer at least thirty of those creations in a fashion book, for lack of a better term. Department stores and dry goods stores are expected to order thousands of books to sell in their establishments or offer for free with a purchase."

"And what's your first impression of the idea?"

"It's a smart marketing tactic, but the novelty will fade fast. Especially since the book isn't exclusive to one store but can be purchased almost anywhere."

"Exactly!" James slapped a hand on his knee. "That's why we plan to outshine them. Our own exclusive publication, out at the same time as theirs."

"That will be quite the endeavor, but if Denwall can afford it, it's brilliant."

"I agree." James smiled and settled back in his seat. "We'd like you to head the project, from the ground up."

Zella blinked. "Me? I've never run a magazine."

"But you *were* the subeditor for one. And from what I understand, you ran more of the day-to-day work than the editor-in-chief did."

Which was why she'd eventually left.

James laid out his argument, ticking off each point on the fingers of his right hand. "You have the experience, the eye for detail, and the editorial sense to make this more than just another catalogue."

"I'm flattered." That was an understatement—like calling the Atlantic damp. "You've seen my work?"

"I've followed your career since before Will met Ivy. As a department store owner, it's important to keep up with what our customers are reading."

Zella had never imagined anyone but women reading her articles on fashion, home décor, and social etiquette. Still, she needed to keep a level head and not let the flattery cloud her judgment. "Where would I work? I live here, in New York."

"Philadelphia. We'll provide an apartment, and you can keep your place here. Once the book is published, I'm sure you'll want to return home. But you'll do so with a big feather in your cap. I'd imagine you'll be in great demand."

It was an enticing offer. If she made the project a success, she'd surely get future offers from the publications that had snubbed her in the past. "You've certainly thought this through," she murmured.

"I want to make this as appealing as possible," James said.

Zella tapped a finger idly against her chin. "If I do this, I want sole authority. If I'm to make it a success, I need control over the content, the layout, the overall vision."

"You'll have it. Final approval goes to the board."

"And Charles Walraven? Is he in favor of this plan?" She resisted the urge to grimace.

James's lips twitched. "It was his idea."

"Really?"

"He appreciates your work. Said if we're going to do this, it needs to be done right, and that meant hiring someone who won't back down when faced with the inevitable challenges. You have a reputation for ... well, let's say, not tolerating nonsense."

That was one way of putting it.

Zella sat back, considering. She would never have expected Charles Walraven, of all people, to push her name forward.

A smile tugged at her lips. "It does sound interesting," she admitted.

James grinned. "Exactly what I hoped you'd say."

"It's a wonderful opportunity," Myra said. "And from what I've seen of your work, you're ideal for the job."

"Thank you." Zella kept her tone mild. "I'd like to talk to Ivy and her grandmother and see what they think." Although she knew without a doubt they'd encourage her to go. They were probably sick of her complaining about the dullness of her life. And now that Ivy was marrying Will, and he would be living close by until the wedding, Zella wouldn't worry about Ivy and Jemima as much.

James nodded. "We head back to Philadelphia tomorrow, but you can telegram me with your decision by the end of the day, Friday. Do three days give you enough time?"

Her pulse quickened. She didn't need three seconds. This project was exactly the kind of challenge she craved—a chance to make a change. "I think I can come to a decision by then."

THREE

Friday, November 15, 1895
Philadelphia

Bert sank into his chair at Denwall's boardroom table, rolling his sore shoulder as he reached for the morning's agenda.

Exuding effortless control, Harlan Ballard leaned back in what had once been Father's chair at the head of the table. Officially interim chief executive, Harlan now ran the executive meetings. Mid-forties, well-dressed, and smooth as silk, he had the easy charm of a man both respected and well-liked. Despite growing up in a poor neighborhood in New Orleans, he commanded the room like he'd been born to it. His slow Southern drawl gave even sharp pronouncements the warmth of a fireside chat.

James Dennison sat next to Harlan and was the kind of man who could calm a storm with a few well-placed words. The negotiator. The people-man. The one who could walk into the employee lunchroom or a Fifth Avenue drawing room and speak both languages fluently. He'd never wanted the full reins of the company, preferring to travel, to nurture partnerships, and to keep his name on every major deal without living under the weight of the daily grind.

Smart man.

James managed to stay essential without being shackled to the top seat. He maintained a balance Bert appreciated and strived for himself. Only he preferred numbers to people. At least he could get them to add up.

Harlan leaned forward and rapped a knuckle on the table. "All right, gentlemen, we have a great deal to cover, so let's get to it."

Max Dennison, James's only son, took the lead. Like his father, he was a charmer and fit perfectly in his role as head of sales. "I have the latest numbers in regional sales performance. Philadelphia continues to lead, outpacing Chicago by twelve percent this quarter. Pittsburgh dipped slightly in October but is rebounding nicely in November, thanks to the early Christmas promotions. We're only a month into the opening of the New York store, but things look very promising."

"New York's first month outperformed expectations," Will interjected. "Foot traffic on Fifth Avenue is strong, and we've seen a sharp uptick in apparel and imported housewares."

Bert nodded slowly. "That's all encouraging, but the Fifth Avenue overhead is still steep. I'd like to see whether the buzz holds through spring before we call it a win." He flicked a look at his brother. "No offense."

"None taken. I'm used to your 'glass is half empty' attitude." Will said this with a smile that told Bert he really wasn't bothered by the remark.

"Naturally, we need to be cautious," Harlan added. "But we'd be fools not to acknowledge a strong opening." He glanced at Tom Morton, head of Denwall's logistics. "Anything new to report, Tom?"

"We're still seeing shipping delays out of the Chicago

warehouse. And we've had a temporary backlog in Pittsburgh." Tom drummed his pen against his agenda. "The issue isn't shipping it's intake. Outdated protocols at the receiving docks. We flagged it last quarter."

"Let's make it a priority." Harlan tapped his forefinger on the table. "Work with Bert on this. I want a plan to review by Monday."

Bert grunted in assent. Another fire to put out.

Will shifted and placed his forearms on the table. "Before we move on, I'd like to mention the One Gown, One Girl campaign launching next week. It's in partnership with the Working Women's Aid Society. Customers can donate gently worn garments for young women entering the workforce. The kickoff luncheon will be held in New York, with a second in Philadelphia."

Harlan steepled his fingers. "Smart public goodwill and timed well for Christmas. Excellent work, Will."

"I can't take the credit, I'm afraid. It was my fiancé's idea. She's seen the need firsthand. Knows what it's like for a young woman who's on her own and must earn a living. It's enough just to keep a roof over her head, let alone buy clothes.

"Brains as well as good looks. No wonder you're marrying her." Max leaned back and grinned. "Can't figure out what she sees in you, however."

A ripple of chuckles moved through the room. Even Bert's mouth twitched. But truthfully, he envied Will just a bit. Ivy was a special person, and his brother was blessed to have her.

Harlan shuffled through the stack of papers in front of him. "Now on to our upcoming spring catalog showcasing European fashion."

The shift in tone was subtle, but the weight behind it unmistakable.

"I'm pleased to announce that Mrs. Zella Capp, the

popular lady correspondent, will be this important project's managing director.

Bert froze mid-reach for his coffee.

Zella Capp?

Murmurs of approval broke out around him. Will smiled, and James gave a nod, as if this had always been the obvious choice. He must have approached her at the engagement dinner.

Tom sniggered. "We're trusting a woman with such an important and enormous endeavor? Has she managed a project like this before?"

"I think you know the answer to that, Morton. It's not the type of position given to women. This is new territory, and Denwall is going to lead the way." Harlan's tone brooked no argument. "Mrs. Capp has an excellent reputation and connections in the fashion industry from New York to Venice. Besides, it's time we show our female customers that we have someone at the top who understands their needs and desires."

Bert didn't have a problem with a woman in charge, but from a numbers standpoint, he'd never been on board with the publication to begin with. "We're actually going forward with this project? Despite the cost projections I gave you?"

Harlan eyed him with a level gaze. "That's correct. The decision was finalized weeks ago when you were in New York."

"And the budget? We've just poured a fortune into a new market, and now we're launching a high-end publication?"

"It's a one-time investment, not a recurring liability." Harlan, in his usual calm demeanor, didn't alter the volume of his voice. "With the fashion house book rumored for delivery to stores all over the country, we need to get a jump on them—offer our unique publication, Denwall style."

"And now we're following the crowd?" Bert muttered. "Is this the right time for such an indulgence? The market is still fragile from the financial panic of '93. Should we be encouraging society ladies to bankrupt their husbands over French lace and ivory buttons?"

Harlan sighed like a man worn down by stupid questions. "We are seeing a rebound in the economy, albeit slow. People are looking for something to lift their spirits. Besides, we're not here to pass moral judgment. We're here to anticipate desire. And sell it."

"Zella's the right person for this. She knows the market. She knows how to tell a story," Will added.

It figured he would be on the side of hiring Zella. She was Ivy's beloved aunt.

Bert exhaled hard.

Zella.

A woman who could talk a starving man out of his last loaf of bread and make him laugh about it.

"Let's hope she can meet deadlines," Tom said.

"I've no doubt she will." Harlan's voice sharpened. "And I expect full cooperation from everyone in this room."

Bert didn't answer. He just reached for his coffee and took a gulp.

The bitterness suited him.

Four

The Gladstone Apartment House, located on Pine and Eleventh, was situated in a well-connected area of Philadelphia. Within minutes, Zella could catch an electrified streetcar to the Denwall offices on Chestnut, or to the market, as well as numerous museums and libraries. She could even get to the newly built Broad Street Station and hop a train to New York, if she got lonely.

One of the few apartments near enough to Denwall, the Gladstone had only been built in the past three years. Zella appreciated its modern features, including a fire suppression system and a large refrigeration unit. It was a building for the well-to-do—four stories of refinement, offering its residents both elegance and luxury. Denwall had spared no expense in securing her new residence, and as she entered, she could already tell it had been prepared with efficiency and taste.

The parlor was elegantly appointed with high-end but not ostentatious furniture. A velvet chaise in a rich sapphire hue sat beneath tall windows that overlooked the tree-lined Pine Street below. The chairs were upholstered in brocade, the dark wood gleaming from a fresh oiling. A Persian rug stretched across the floor, soft beneath Zella's boots, and the mahogany dining table sat ready for meals she wasn't entirely sure she'd bother to host.

She set down a small box of her belongings, taking in the space. The apartment was furnished with all the essentials. Everything she needed, yet very little of *herself*. The only items she'd brought from Manhattan were a few books, some clothing, and the small wooden box that now sat open on the side table, filled with loose odds and ends from her trips abroad with Florence.

Ivy had generously taken the day off from her bookshop to accompany her. "To help you get settled in," she'd said. Will had already been in town for a few days, so Zella suspected Ivy's eagerness to join her wasn't entirely altruistic.

Truth be told, Zella wasn't used to accepting help, but Ivy took charge the moment they arrived, bustling about and unpacking as if she meant to stay herself. Will stood by the fireplace, surveying the room with a satisfied nod.

"Your assistant thought of everything," he said.

Zella hadn't had the luxury to choose her assistant herself, but James had assured her that Sylvia Leighton was top-notch. Will moved to help Ivy lift a box to the dining room table. She cut through the twine and went to work while Zella unpacked her writing utensils and set them on a roll-top desk.

"Where would you like this picture to go?"

Zella pivoted to see Ivy holding a small velvet-covered frame that held the picture of a man in his mid-twenties. His expression was serious, his suit well-tailored, but there was nothing striking about him. Nothing that caused her breath to quicken, or her heart to patter.

Because Zella had never actually met him.

She took the frame from Ivy's hand and ran a thumb along its soft edges. *Jeremiah Capp. Her late husband.*

At least, that's what everyone thought.

The truth was more tangled. The man in the picture had been the beau of her first roommate in Chicago. When the roommate tossed the picture into the trash bin and moved to San Francisco, Zella had recovered it, and the made-up story of her married life began. The name had come from a tonic water label—Cappella's Tonic for Nerves and Vitality, which she shortened to Capp, and just like that, Jeremiah Capp existed.

She swallowed against the tightening in her throat. It had been thirteen years since she had invented him, since she had let the lie take root. The only people to whom Zella had ever told the truth were her sister, Rosina, and Florence Ashford.

Now frail and fading in Chicago, Florence had listened without judgment. She had been kind, pragmatic even, when Zella confided in her. *You did what you had to, dear. The world is not always fair to a woman on her own.*

But Rosina had been disappointed when she learned of Zella's subterfuge.

Zella could still hear her sister's voice, whispering harshly in the Kings' kitchen above their bookshop. *You lied about something sacred, Zella! You pretended to be a widow. Do you even understand what that means?*

Of course she'd understood.

It meant security. It meant no questions about why she was unmarried. Magazines hired her because of it. No editor would have believed an unmarried woman in her early twenties could write about how to manage a house or pick out appropriate fashions. A woman who'd never married certainly couldn't visit exotic countries and write about the lives of women in China or Japan.

And more than anything, Zella had wanted to write those types of articles.

But that didn't mean she didn't feel the weight of the lie now.

She exhaled and set the photo aside. One day soon, she'd tell Ivy the truth.

Just not right now.

Ivy's voice pulled her from her thoughts. "You look lost in your head."

Zella forced a smile. "Just thinking about how ridiculous Jeremiah's mustache was."

"It *is* rather tragic." Ivy turned back to the table and unwrapped the remaining frames. One of Ivy with her parents, and one of Florence.

"How is Mrs. Ashford?" Ivy asked as she took in the face of a woman who exuded the self-confidence afforded by wealth and social status.

Zella's stomach clenched. She should write and arrange a visit to Chicago. Florence had been good to her, had been her mentor and friend, and she deserved more than a monthly letter and a semi-annual visit. "The last I heard, she's doing well, but she's frail. I worry about her."

"Didn't you tell me she has a son?"

Zella huffed. "Quentin. A man with no ambition but to live off his mother." She just hoped that he was at least looking after Florence. Not in a financial way, as she didn't need money, but in an emotional way.

As soon as she could get away, Zella would make a weekend visit to Chicago. When that would be, however, she hadn't a clue. The task of publishing a hefty multi-country publication would take every waking moment.

"I can't believe I start at Denwall tomorrow."

James had made the offer to her only eight days before.

Will chuckled. "Once we make up our minds to do something, we don't dawdle. In this business, if you take your time you'll be trampled by the competition."

Zella understood this. It was how she lived her life.

Bert spent the first hour of the morning in a meeting with Max regarding the feasibility of giving their buyers a raise. His secretary slipped in and set a crisp memo on his desk.

Actually, it was more like a summons. Harlan and James were both traveling, which meant someone had to introduce Mrs. Capp to the inner workings of the company. And by *someone*, apparently, that meant him.

Max shrugged. "I could take her around for you."

Bert didn't like the gleam in his friend's eye. Max was an incorrigible flirt. It was Bert's duty, as Ivy's future brother-in-law, to look after her aunt.

"It's fine. I'll handle it. Shouldn't take long."

Max snickered and rose to his feet. "Good luck, my friend."

Bert pushed back from his desk and reluctantly walked out the door. He took the elevator from the sixth floor to the lobby of Denwall's office building that sat next to their first and largest store.

And there was Zella.

She stood near the window, silhouetted against the light, dressed in a smart, deep green walking suit with brass buttons, and a hat perched at a rakish angle. She appeared far too comfortable for someone stepping into an unfamiliar job.

She turned her head at the sound of his approach, her smile immediate and knowing.

Bert wasn't sure which was more irritating, being forced to interrupt his morning for Zella's orientation or that she seemed utterly delighted to have him at her mercy. The last thing he needed was another distraction when more pressing matters were at hand.

"I wondered who Mr. Ballard would rope into tour guide duty."

Bert swallowed a sigh, forcing his tone into civility. "I'm afraid my schedule today is rather tight."

She tilted her head playfully. "And yet, here you are."

"Not by choice," he grumbled. Bert straightened, forcing himself into the role of reluctant escort. "Let's get this over with."

He placed a light hand on her elbow and guided her to the elevator, directing the operator to take them down. "We house our publications department in the basement, where there's ample space. The department was an addition several years ago when the cost of sending out our catalogues to a publishing firm became astronomical."

Zella quirked a brow. "Your idea, I assume?"

"I'm always a proponent of cost-saving measures."

"But not at the expense of quality, I hope."

"It's a balance." Bert could already tell that this was going to be a point of contention between them—his desire to keep costs at or below budget and her desire to produce an eye-catching, and perhaps extravagant, publication.

When they stepped off the elevator, the scent of fresh ink and crisp paper hung thick in the air, blending with beeswax polish and the subtle lavender fragrance often favored by female staff. The place was efficient and bright, with high windows letting in the hazy morning light. Rows of desks stretched in neat formation, already occupied by copywriters and illustrators.

"This is our main publications department," Bert waved a hand, "although we have smaller ones in all our department stores for day-to-day ad copy. Editorial desks are on the left. Illustrators on the right. Engraving and printing coordination is handled in the space down the hall. And through here—" he gestured toward an oak-framed glass door "—is your office."

Zella moved past him, pushing open the door with an air of satisfaction. The space was generous for someone new to the company, complete with a massive desk, an elegant settee against the wall, and a bookshelf already lined with volumes on European fashion and art.

"Well," she said, smoothing her glove over the polished surface of the desk, "I have to admit, someone did a fine job of preparing the space."

Bert grunted. "I'm sure it was your assistant." At the sound of someone stepping through the office doorway, Bert glanced over his shoulder. "Ah, here's Miss Leighton now."

Hand-picked by Ballard himself, Miss Leighton was precisely the type of person he'd expect the chief executive to choose—sharp, well-mannered, and immaculately dressed, her navy skirt suit tailored to perfection. Her dark blonde hair was pinned in a soft but precise twist, and her hands held a leather portfolio against her chest as she surveyed Zella with polite curiosity.

"Mrs. Capp," Miss Leighton said warmly. "I'm Sylvia Leighton. I'll be your secretary."

Zella extended her hand. "It's good to meet you, Miss Leighton. I'm glad to have you on board."

"I've already taken the liberty of organizing the office's correspondence. You have a stack of inquiries waiting on your desk. I've set up a filing system for you and began marking up your calendar with appointments."

"You're very efficient," Zella said.

Miss Leighton nodded and smiled. "I like things in order."

Zella's grey eyes flicked to Bert, and he shrugged. "This is Denwall. We don't waste time." He wouldn't get in the middle of the situation, but Miss Leighton's activities were a bit high-handed for someone in her position, especially since she had never worked with Zella.

"Thank you so much for your efforts, Miss Leighton."

Zella straightened her shoulders. "I'm not accustomed to having an assistant, so you'll have to pardon my inexperience. However, I am, shall we say, persnickety about how my things are filed."

She glanced at the watch on her chatelaine. "Let's get together in an hour in my office, and we'll discuss it further. For now, will you please put four receptacles—wire baskets or whatever is available—on my desk? Then we'll prepare to get to work the day after Thanksgiving."

Miss Leighton tipped her head. "Certainly, Mrs. Capp. And I completely understand. I'll do whatever you need to make your work environment pleasing."

When the assistant had walked away, Bert turned to Zella and grinned. "You like to be in control." It wasn't a question.

"Of course." Zella narrowed her eyes and pointed a finger at him. "And don't make it sound so negative. I imagine you're one who likes things done a certain way too."

He'd never thought about it, but he supposed she was correct. "I like to be prepared for any situation. And I don't like surprises, especially in the company's numbers."

She slipped her arm through his and whispered, "Well, that may cause some fireworks down the road. But I can handle confrontation now and again."

Why did Bert have the sinking feeling he'd have confrontations with Zella more frequently than *now and again*?

FIVE

Thanksgiving didn't rank high on Zella's list of special days because it was one of the last times she'd seen her parents. She and Mam had spent the entire day roasting the turkey and making sure that all Da's favorite dishes were on the table. Instead of gratitude, however, he berated and belittled them for one thing after another.

Worse than that was his lecture about how she would marry farmer Matthews to *mutually benefit* their two farms. He wouldn't take no for an answer.

Before the Christmas tree was trimmed, eighteen-year-old Zella packed her bags and left their small Ohio farm in the middle of the night.

Never to return.

Needless to say, when James Dennison stopped by her office to invite her to join his family for Thanksgiving, her first instinct was to refuse. But she realized not only would it be a horrible career choice to say no, but that James was not her father. She'd seen him with his family and doubted he'd berate them over anything.

So, Zella dressed that morning in her prettiest autumn

visiting toilette and hired a hansom cab to drive her to Rittenhouse Square.

She alighted from the cab, her gaze drifting up the brownstone façade of the Dennison mansion. Warm gaslight flickered beside the carved doorway, catching in the polished glass of the transom window etched with the family's monogram. A gust of wind stirred the ivy clinging to the wrought-iron fence, rustling the last of the golden leaves in the garden. As she climbed the sweeping front steps, a knot of apprehension coiled in her chest.

The door opened before she could knock, and a liveried butler greeted her with a dignified nod, relieving her of her gloves and coat. "Mrs. Capp, welcome."

The marble-tiled foyer gleamed under the chandelier's soft glow. Gilt-framed mirrors reflected the elegance of the damask wallpaper and the gentle curve of the mahogany staircase. From the drawing room beyond came the sound of laughter and a few off-key notes from the piano.

Zella was shown in with the grace and assurance of a longtime retainer. The drawing room exuded rococo elegance with its pale blue and ivory walls, gold leaf accents, silk settees, and a fire flickering beneath the marble mantel. The air smelled faintly of beeswax, roses, and something sweet baking in the kitchen. James and Myra sat in a matching pair of high-backed Queen Anne chairs, while five young adults took up the two damask settees in the room.

Elegant in sapphire silk, Myra rose to greet Zella first, with two of her stepdaughters close behind.

Zella had met the entire Dennison family at the grand opening of Denwall's New York store, but the introductions had been so quick, she didn't remember a single name, except the son's.

"Mrs. Capp, we're delighted you could come," Myra said

brightly. "You'd probably rather be with your own parents, but we hope we're a good stand-in."

Zella took Myra's outstretched hand and gave it a light squeeze. In truth, she'd prefer postponing a Thanksgiving reunion with her parents—especially since they'd both died of the influenza three years after she moved to Chicago.

Myra slipped her arm through hers and pointed to each of the people in the room. "Helena is our oldest daughter. Then there are Louise and Beatrice. Alexandra is our youngest child. And Max is our only son, and the oldest of the five."

The resemblance between the Dennison children was undeniable. All with varying shades of red hair, and all with blue eyes, except maybe the youngest. From a few feet away, Zella thought her eyes might be green.

Helena, Beatrice, Louise, and Alexandra. Hmmm.

"You wouldn't happen to be named after Queen Victoria's daughters, would you?"

Laughter broke out, and James pointed to the youngest. "All but Alix, here. She's named after Prince Edward's wife."

Zella smiled at the young woman, who was probably only seventeen or eighteen and possessed the straightest teeth she'd ever seen. "Did you say *Alex*?"

Alexandra shook her head. "My nickname is Alix, A-L-I-X because that's what Papa says the Princess of Wales is called by her family and closest friends."

"I refuse to call my daughters by their royal names in case they get big heads. My late wife, an Englishwoman by birth, gave them their names." James pointed a thumb at his chest. "But I gave them their nicknames."

Interesting. "And what are those nicknames, pray tell?"

"Lena, Tris, Lou, and, of course, Alix."

Zella tapped a forefinger against her chin and shifted her gaze to Max. "And Max? Is that short for Maxwell? Honestly, I don't recall a Maxwell among Victoria's brood."

The room erupted in laughter, and Max shrugged a shoulder. "No, it's just Max. I was named after my mother's beloved childhood dog."

Zella couldn't hold back a snort, and she placed a hand over her mouth. "Oh, I'm so sorry. I don't mean to laugh. But *that* is a great story."

Max stuck his hands in his pockets and grinned. "Let's keep it out of your articles, shall we?"

"Mum's the word."

The Dennisons took their seats, and Alexandra patted the spot next to her on one of the settees. "Sit here, Mrs. Capp."

"Please, call me Zella."

Helena, who sat on Zella's other side, tilted her head. "Zella is such an unusual name."

"My mother loved Mary Shelley's books. I was named after Zella in the short story 'The Evil Eye' and my sister Rosina from *The Invisible Girl*."

"I've only read *Frankenstein*." Myra shuddered. "Too frightening for my tastes."

Zella wasn't too fond of it, either.

After a few minutes of light conversation, a soft chime echoed from the hallway, and the butler reappeared at the door.

"Dinner is served."

Max extended an arm to Zella. "Shall we?"

Ivy had warned Zella that Max was a consummate flirt, but she accepted his offer. They followed the family through a wide arched doorway into the formal dining room, a fussy room with wallpaper depicting scenes of pastoral France and paintings hung on every available wall space.

Footmen pulled back velvet dining chairs, and Zella took the vacant seat next to Helena. The servants returned with platters full of more food than one family could eat, and soon the rich aroma of roasted turkey and spiced yams filled the air.

The spirited energy around the table bordered on chaotic. There were mild discussions about fashion and the latest Philadelphia gossip, and heated ones about sports and politics.

As the meal progressed, Zella observed the Dennison family dynamic unfold around her like a well-rehearsed play. It was a mixture of warm familiarity, sharp wit, and undeniable affection.

Beatrice was opinionated and relentless, especially on the subject of fashion reform, launching into an impassioned argument about the horrors of tight-laced corsets.

"Women should be able to take a deep breath, don't you think?" she asked, turning to Zella, as if she were petitioning a judge for an important ruling.

Zella set down her fork, considering. "Breathing is certainly a luxury worth fighting for."

Louise—Zella was amazed her family got away with calling her Lou—was the quietest and most observant of the bunch. "Careful, Zella. If you agree with Tris on one thing, she'll make you march in a suffrage parade next."

"That reminds me," Beatrice said, brightening. "Do you support women's suffrage, Zella?"

"I'd hardly be writing articles about the New Woman if I thought they shouldn't vote, don't you think?"

Max let out a warm laugh, leaning back in his chair. "Now, that was well played."

The conversation shifted to the merits of London versus New York fashion, with Myra insisting that the only true refinement came from across the Atlantic.

"I must introduce you to some of my dear friends who share their homes between London and Philadelphia," Myra said to Zella between bites of creamed onions. "A feature on British fashion will undoubtedly elevate the magazine."

"Oh, certainly," Beatrice said dryly, buttering her roll.

"Because American women are just desperate to be told how inferior they are."

Helena slowly shook her head, while Alexandra leaned in, eyes bright with curiosity.

"Will there be a feature on debutante fashion?"

"Let me guess—you have a vested interest in debuts?" Zella smiled at Alexandra's hopeful expression.

"Just a bit."

James groaned. "Both Alix and Caroline Walraven are coming out this season."

"Heaven help us," Max added, sending Alexandra a wink from across the table. His easygoing smile could probably cajole the grumpiest of individuals and cause most women, who weren't his sisters, to swoon.

For Zella, not as much.

It wasn't that Max wasn't charming. He was. And hand-some. And easy to talk to, even if he was only twenty-nine. Four years her junior. If Zella had ever entertained thoughts of marriage, he would be the sort of man she might have sought.

But she didn't seek a man. And she never would.

She knew too well what it meant to be under a man's thumb. Just look at Mam. And love—if it truly existed—wasn't a foundation she could trust.

Instead of lingering on the thought, she turned to Alexandra. "I'll take all your opinions under advisement," she said in a serious tone.

James chuckled, shaking his head. "You have no idea what you've signed up for, Zella."

Zella's lips twitched. She was starting to think that maybe she did.

And that wasn't such a bad thing.

It was Thanksgiving as it had always been at the Walraven home. The dining room was set to perfection with its long, polished table gleaming under the glow of the chandelier. The rich scent of roasted turkey, chestnut stuffing, and mulled cider filled the air.

But it wasn't the same.

Bert turned his gaze to the empty chair beside him.

For the first Thanksgiving in almost thirty years, Will wasn't with the family. The son who'd always been the one to bend to Father's wishes—until he met Ivy—had chosen to return to New York to spend the day with Ivy and her grandmother.

It made sense, of course. Will worked full time in New York now. He and Ivy were engaged and building their own life. But still ...

Tradition had been broken, and the weight of it settled uneasily in Bert's chest.

Last year, he and Will had shared the turkey carving duties. Father seemed pale that day, and though he'd brushed it off as indigestion, Mother had exchanged a look with Bert that said otherwise. The doctors hadn't diagnosed the heart condition yet, but Mother must have suspected something was wrong. Will had challenged Bert to a carving competition to determine the best carver in the family. But Bert was a precision man, and Mother declared his slices the most uniform.

They'd all laughed at Will's act of dejection. Even Father managed a smile.

Now Will's chair stood empty, and the turkey had been carved in the kitchen by Cook.

"You're quiet tonight."

Bert glanced up to see Ned watching him curiously from across the table. Fresh-faced and full of university confidence, he looked like a young version of their father—but with far less gravitas, more reckless enthusiasm, and their mother's coloring. Bert predicted his youngest brother would be the first of Charles Walraven's sons to fly the Denwall coop.

Bert reached for the carved turkey slices before him and shrugged a shoulder at Ned's observation. "Just strange, that's all."

Ned smirked. "Strange that Will's not here? Or strange that you're the one stuck here while he's off planning his wedding?"

Seated in the dining chair next to Ned, Caroline arched a brow. "He's not *stuck*, Ned."

Bert gave her a grateful glance. "Thank you, Caro."

"Besides, if anyone's *stuck* with family obligations, it's me." She sighed, setting down her fork. "The debutante season is exhausting."

Ned took a bite of sweet potatoes and spoke around it, "Not finding enough eager suitors?"

Caroline shot him a flat look. "None that I don't tower over."

It was true. Caroline was taller than most of the men her age, and though she carried herself with grace, Bert knew her height made her self-conscious. Alix Dennison, her best friend, had no such concerns. For reasons he failed to understand, society looked more favorably upon petite women.

Mother, ever poised and thoughtful, reached for Caroline's hand. "The season's only just started. The Lord has the perfect man in mind for you. You just need to be still and wait on Him."

Caroline didn't look convinced, but before she could argue, Father cleared his throat.

"Let's not think about marriage yet, Caroline. We're not ready for you to leave us anytime soon."

Hands down, Caroline was Father's favorite child. Probably because she was the only girl. He certainly didn't belittle anything she did, nor expect her life to be subservient to Denwall.

Father shifted his dark eyes to Bert. "What do you think of Mrs. Capp? I thought she was an excellent choice to head our new endeavor and suggested her to James."

Bert nearly choked on his potatoes. "You suggested her?"

"Of course. She's sharp, has a flair women admire, and knows enough about the business to make the publication a success."

"She's unpredictable," Bert replied.

Father let out a rare chuckle. "That's exactly why she's the right choice." He leaned forward slightly, his tone as measured as always. "A project like this isn't just about selling fashion. It's about building something memorable that will keep Denwall at the forefront of shoppers' minds."

Bert's eyes flicked to his mother, expecting her to voice concern. But she only beamed at Father's insightfulness.

"We'll know soon enough if she can handle it," she said, "but my money's on yes."

Ned, easily amused, leaned back and grinned. "It should be interesting."

"How would you know?" Bert asked.

"I met her at the grand opening of the New York store. We actually talked for about twenty minutes. Longest conversation I've ever had with a woman who's not family."

"Other than Alix," Caroline said.

Ned shifted in his chair. "That's different."

Now *that* was interesting.

Caroline peeked at her parents, who were deep in their own conversation, and said in a low voice near Bert's ear. "I love Mrs. Capp's articles. I want to be a writer like her."

Trying to wrap his mind around this piece of news, Bert asked, "You want to be a writer?"

"Not fashion or home décor articles, but essays. Things that matter."

Out of the mouths of babes. "You've never said anything."

"You've never asked." Caroline's tone was mild, but her words hit like a blow. It was true. She was on the cusp of womanhood and had ideas of her own. Ideas of which he hadn't shown any interest.

Before Bert could respond, a servant approached with trays laden with steaming mince pies, apple tarts glazed in cinnamon sugar, and a rich plum pudding crowned with holly and still glistening from the brandy flame.

Father's eyes widened, and he rubbed his hands together. Sweets were his Achilles' heel.

Mother placed a hand on his arm. "Only one dessert, dear."

"Killjoy," Father grumbled.

Conversation ceased as everyone dug into the rich offerings. Cook, it seemed, had outdone herself tonight.

But Bert only picked at his plum pudding, one of his favorite holiday dishes. He stared out the dining room window, which overlooked the park across the street. The street was dark and quiet, everyone inside with their families.

Guilt coiled in his gut.

He should have asked Zella if she had somewhere to go for dinner, but it hadn't even crossed his mind until now. She'd mentioned she had work to do tomorrow, so she wouldn't have time to go to New York for the day.

He doubted she'd want pity, however. She'd snap his head off if he offered it, but he hoped she wasn't alone.

No matter what, he wasn't about to reveal to anyone that he'd been thinking about her.

Six

Zella smoothed her skirt and adjusted the cuff of her jacket, then pressed a steadying hand to her stomach. She'd dressed with care that morning, wanting to project competence and control. A tailored skirt and blouse, paired with a trim jacket, subtly hinted at confidence and authority.

She wasn't nervous, exactly. This wasn't her first time presenting ideas to executives or having her work scrutinized like a bug under a magnifying glass. Five years ago, she'd convinced *Harper's Bazaar* to run a series on the British royal family, from an American woman's perspective, no less. And she'd talked *Vogue* into publishing the daring article she wrote on the need for a healthier approach to women's clothing.

So yes, she had experience dealing with men and their prejudices.

Just not on this scale.

The Denwall boardroom was cavernous, its long walnut table polished to a near-mirror finish. Harlan sat at the head, flanked by Charles on one side—a rare treat, as she understood it—and James on the other. A half dozen other department heads occupied the remaining seats. Behind her stood an easel with several interior book layouts she planned to present to the board.

Bert, who hadn't said a word to her since arriving, was at the far end, arms crossed.

Zella stood at the front of the room, fingers wrapped around a wooden pointer like it was a conductor's baton. She needed to get her point across before she lost these busy men's interest, so she and an in-house illustrator had worked around the clock to come up with a cover design and three interior layouts to present. They'd put together more and then chose the most impactful three.

Harlan rapped his knuckles on the table and rose. "Thank you all for coming and for being prompt. We have Mrs. Capp with us this morning. As you know, she is the managing director of our European fashions catalog, which is slated for publication in early April. She's here to present her ideas for the publication. Please give her your full attention. Since time is of the essence, we'll not leave tonight until we've made a final decision on the layout." He turned to Zella and tipped his head. "The floor is yours, Mrs. Capp."

"Thank you, Mr. Ballard. And thank you all for your time this morning. I'll be brief."

That wasn't entirely true. She intended to be persuasive. Thorough. Irrefutable.

"As you know, Denwall's original concept was a fashion catalog featuring European styles that could be adapted for apparel sold in Denwall stores. You envisioned a publication that would compete with the fashion house collaborative coming out this spring, which my reliable sources tell me will be titled *Coming Styles Designed by the Great Costumers of Europe*, and will contain thirty unique fashion prints from fashion houses across the pond."

Murmurs rippled through the room.

Zella's lips turned up. "Yes, it's a high bar to overcome.

However, we shouldn't offer a publication that merely rivals it —but one that outshines it. We don't want the market talking about *that* collaboration. We want them talking about Denwall. I believe there's an opportunity here to go beyond the product listings of a catalog and offer our customers something in tune with their dreams. An illustrated book that functions as both style guide and keepsake."

Bert shifted in his seat, but Zella refused to glance his way. Instead, she passed out a proposal packet to each board member so they could review it again after the presentation.

"I propose we title our publication *Denwall's European Styles Book.*" She flipped the first page on the easel to reveal a penciled mockup of a woman dressed in a ballgown, with the silhouettes of couples swirling on a ballroom floor and a handsome man gazing at her.

"Our customers don't just want the toilette. They want the lifestyle that goes with it. The parlors, the fine china, the silverware. The seaside holidays. The grand debut for their daughters." Zella's eyes met every man in the room. "Women spend hours reading *Godey's* not because they need new wallpaper, but because it makes them feel like they belong to a better world. We're not selling products—we're selling aspiration."

She flipped to an interior layout featuring a fashionable woman in a tailored jacket, striped skirt, and a straw hat perched at a jaunty angle. A tennis racket rested on her shoulder, her profile caught in mid-stride.

"Articles will support the advertisements," Zella continued. "A feature on the benefits of tennis, for example, could include an illustration like this one and a product photograph of our rackets manufactured by Slazenger in England. Or a column on proper travel attire, alongside the newest trunk collection by Louis Vuitton in France."

Executives bobbed their heads. Some scribbled notes on the outlines she'd provided.

Zella took a deep breath. At least no one had fallen asleep.

One layout remained. Without a doubt, this would be the section that drew the most dissent. "We'll also have a home goods section. I know this was not in the plan, but hear me out before you pass judgment."

A few men frowned, and Zella wondered—not for the first time—if any of them had ever taken direction from a woman.

No matter. She had a job to do, and so she pressed on. "Featured articles will include trends in home décor. I plan to gain access to some well-heeled estates through my connections in Europe. We'll have illustrations of their public rooms —from entryways to parlors and dining rooms. And we'll feature full-page layouts to entice American customers to buy similar household goods that we carry at Denwall." She paused and caught Max Dennison's gaze. "We'll need to see your plans for inventory over the coming months."

Charles Walraven cleared his throat. "It sounds ambitious."

"Perhaps. But I've never been one to stop at the clouds when there are stars to chase."

Laughter flitted through the room.

"Do you have cost figures?" Harlan asked.

"Almost."

"Get with Robert when you're ready," Harlan said. "Once you're both in agreement, we'll meet again to vote on the final budget."

There was a beat of silence. Tom Morton, the logistics manager, leaned back in his chair. By his posture, Zella knew his question would be snarky.

"This sounds like a pretty parlor-table book. How will it

get customers in our stores? I'm not sure I see the connection. Seems like you're encouraging reading, not buying."

"On the contrary," she said. "It'll bring them in. Over and over. The longer they spend with our *Styles Book*, the more they'll notice what they're missing. Mark my words, they'll bring that book with them to their nearest Denwall store—and they'll shop from the page."

Someone chuckled. "You sound like one of the copywriters already."

Zella allowed herself a smile.

Then Bert finally cleared his throat, and her stomach clenched. "And what if it flops?" His voice was mild, but every eye turned to him.

Stick-in-the-mud.

Zella pulled her shoulders back and set her eyes on him. "It won't." Someone had once told her that when she was determined about something, her gray eyes took on the glint of steel.

Bert's jaw worked. He didn't reply.

Harlan glanced around the room. "Any further questions?"

There were a few questions about page count and circulation estimates. She answered them all as concisely and confidently as she could muster. By the time her presentation ended, several men around the table were nodding with genuine interest. Harlan reminded them he needed their final vote on the layout by the end of the day.

Bert had said little. But as he rose, he gathered her proposal packet and tapped it neatly on the table. His mouth was pressed into a line.

"Well then. Looks like you've done your homework." His voice carried just enough surprise to be gratifying.

Zella nodded once. "I usually do."

Bert walked back to his office with Zella's voice still echoing in his ears.

Not just the words, but the cadence of them. Steady. Confident. Almost musical in its rhythm, like she'd rehearsed the entire pitch down to the moment she smiled and caught Max off guard with a direct request.

She'd controlled that meeting and not with theatrics. Not with the overly sweet tone some women used when asking for approval in a room full of men, and certainly not with flirtation. Zella, with her natural femininity and attractiveness, had no need for that. It had even bothered him a bit that she hadn't glanced his way more than twice.

Truth be told, she had controlled the presentation with clarity, composure, and facts, which Bert admired above all else. He was a numbers man, not easily swayed by dramatics or nebulous projections.

Although he hadn't expected her to fail, Bert also hadn't expected to be so impressed. Which didn't sit well. Neither did the fact that his mind had wandered from her presentation to her person a few times. The way her professional-looking maroon jacket and skirt couldn't hide her feminine curves. How her lovely gray eyes glinted with steely determination and that she always wore a mourning brooch with every outfit. Although he didn't want to be caught staring at her chest, he'd looked long enough to know that the brooch held two photographs, one of a woman who had to be her sister, and the other of a man. Her husband, perhaps?

What sort of man would catch Zella's interest enough to marry?

Not soft. That much seemed obvious. Not timid or self-important or overly traditional. Someone strong enough not to be threatened by her ambition, but sharp enough not to underestimate her. Bert rubbed the back of his neck. If such a man existed, he'd need to be clever and resilient.

He stepped into his office and shut the door behind him, letting it close with a quiet click. At his desk, he set down the presentation summary Zella had given all the executives and flipped through the mockups again.

Clean lines. Thoughtful placement. A tone that felt just aspirational enough to sell a dream without making it untouchable. The penciled table of contents indicated that each section would lead into the next with the kind of cohesion he would have expected from a seasoned editorial team.

She'd deflected Harlan's question about the budget, but she must have some idea of how much this project was going to cost Denwall, and Bert should've asked more questions. That was his role, after all—to keep projects like this grounded. Accountable.

Instead, he'd found himself watching the way she held the pointer. The way her hand moved with purpose, her shoulders back, her chin tilted just so. She'd looked more like a professor than a department manager. And she hadn't played the martyr, either. There was no mention of late nights or extra work or what she'd given up to get this far.

She'd simply stood there and told them what she planned to do, then showed them how she'd do it. With polish. With poise. With an air of certainty that made him forget, for a moment, that this whole endeavor had once struck him as ridiculous.

And he'd sat there, arms crossed like a pouting schoolboy, while she managed to win him over to her way of thinking. At least, partially. More than where he'd been when he walked into the meeting. He didn't want to admit it out loud yet, but the *Styles Book* had a chance. Not just to succeed, but to redefine their future marketing efforts.

He ran a hand down his face and let out a low sigh.

Maybe what surprised him most was himself—and the fact that he wasn't rooting against her anymore. Somewhere between the cover and Zella's declaration that the project wouldn't fail, he'd crossed a line he hadn't even known he'd drawn.

He was rooting for her. Just a little.

Blast it all.

Bert leaned forward again, tugged open the top drawer of his desk, and retrieved a pencil. He scribbled a few notes in the margin of her packet that included questions about print quantities, travel expenses, and binding requirements. He was still head of finance. It was his job to ask hard questions. And he was going to make her prove every number.

But he was also going to stop underestimating her.

Because the truth was—whether he liked it or not—Zella Capp might just know what she was doing.

And if she didn't?

Well ... she'd go down swinging.

He could respect that.

SEVEN

Zella tapped her pencil against her open notebook, considering the list of tasks before her. On her first day in the Denwall offices, she'd meticulously calculated and recorded what she needed to accomplish each step of the way to deliver a spectacular *Denwall's European Styles Book* by April sixth.

Two weeks into the project, they were on track.

The concept presentation to the board was behind her, and there were tentative layouts and storyboards sketched in pencil for her to review.

They'd agreed on an eighty-page book to start, along with decisions on the dedicated columns: fashion, seasonal etiquette, and a spotlight on emerging trends in home décor—what one of the in-house copywriters had charmingly dubbed "Modern Domesticities."

Zella had even roughed in a short story—something with a governess and an earl for their female audience, if they could secure a reliable and talented fiction writer. If not, she'd simply write it herself under a pen name. She'd done stranger things for a byline.

She'd heard from several well-known freelance writers who

would cost a pretty penny to secure, but she'd also heard from many younger talents willing to write for exposure. In addition, she'd priced out sewn binding instead of wire. More expensive, yes, but durable and elegant. The publication would be a keepsake, not a throwaway. She wanted women to read the *Styles Book*, save it, and lend it to their sisters.

Before she could do anything else, she needed to present a budget to the board, which must first be approved by Bert.

Zella knew how these things worked. Executives said yes in principle, then sliced the budget in half when faced with what the best would cost them.

And that wouldn't do. This wasn't just another Denwall circular.

Potentially locking horns with Bert wasn't the only problem facing her. She had also failed to establish a rapport with her team. There were times she felt like she was trying to muster unwilling troops before a battle.

She'd noticed the whispers. The side glances. It was the sort of atmosphere she recognized immediately. Not outright resistance, but subtle undercurrents of doubt. Some of the staff were surely questioning her abilities. Maybe even undermining her without realizing it.

It wasn't as if they ignored her outright, but there was a deliberate slowness in response times, a lack of urgency in meetings, and the distinct feeling that decisions were being debated behind closed doors.

Zella took a deep breath, forcing herself to remain composed.

She wasn't a paranoiac. But she knew when people talked behind her back. She had spent years navigating the world of publishing as well as the world in general as an unmarried woman, despite posing as a widow.

At least she had Miss Leighton, who sometimes seemed like Zella's only ally. She consistently greeted Zella with a smile, offered to get her coffee, and was always meticulously prepared with schedule updates and organized notes. She even adapted to Zella's sorting system, which consisted of four wire baskets, one each for incoming illustrations, copy, correspondence, and proposals.

Zella sat forward, flipping through a stack of notes Miss Leighton had left on her desk that morning. Everything Zella needed to deliver a budget to Bert, meticulously typed and labeled. Estimates for in-house illustration costs, copywriting hours, ink and plate preparation, even travel stipends for potential fashion correspondents.

Except the most critical piece was missing.

The estimate from Astor and Halston Printing.

Zella frowned. They had been waiting for confirmation on printing estimates for over a week.

Pushing back from her desk, she left her office and strode across the main floor toward Miss Leighton's desk. The clatter of typewriters, the scratch of pen against paper, and the low hum of voices filled the space.

As she neared, Miss Leighton was already looking up.

"Mrs. Capp," she said smoothly, setting down her fountain pen. "Do you need something?"

"Did we receive the final estimate from Astor and Halston?"

Miss Leighton hesitated for the briefest moment. "Yes, don't you remember? I put it on your desk a few days ago."

No, she didn't remember the secretary mentioning it, let alone seeing it on her desk. She'd not been sleeping well the past few days. Did that account for her memory loss?

"I'll double-check my baskets."

Miss Leighton tilted her head. "Maybe you filed it already."

Forgetting it arrived on her desk and that she'd filed it?

Zella hoped that wasn't the case. Still, she needed to find the estimate soon.

She pivoted on her heels to head back to her office and bumped directly into Bert's secretary.

"Mr. Walraven would like to see you, Mrs. Capp. He's asked that you bring your budget."

Blast it all. The timing couldn't be worse.

"Right now?" If she had a few minutes, she could search for and presumably find the printing estimate.

"Yes, right now, please. He has a meeting to attend across town and can't wait."

Her heart thudded. She couldn't very well present a budget without the printing estimate—it was the lion's share of the cost. She could ask to reschedule, plead disorganization, but the idea was revolting.

Zella Capp didn't shrink from scrutiny. She'd go in with the best version she had. And sell it like a ribbon vendor at a county fair.

The elevator dinged.

Through the door he'd left open on purpose, Bert watched Zella as she stepped into the corridor. Her gaze hadn't met his yet, so he was able to watch her a little longer than he would have otherwise.

He'd sent his secretary to ask her up to the sixth floor to discuss the budget they would present to the board next week.

She tucked a leather portfolio tighter under her arm and squared her shoulders, as if bracing for a duel. The click of her shoes on the marble floor increased in volume as she approached Bert's office.

Bert quickly looked down at his desk and then realized

there was nothing in front of him to look at. He shifted a stack of papers into his field of vision and furrowed his brow in mock concentration.

Zella knocked once on the open door.

Bert lifted his head and stood. "Good afternoon, Mrs. Capp." It wouldn't do for the staff to hear them on familiar terms, even if they were to be in-laws next year. *Is that what she'd be? His aunt-in-law?* He almost laughed out loud.

"Won't you have a seat? Did you bring your budget figures?" He tried valiantly to sound stern, which he most definitely was when it came to money.

She nodded and took the seat in front of his desk.

"So, tell me." He folded his long frame into his leather chair. "Are your numbers as ridiculous as I've heard rumored?"

Zella placed her portfolio on his desk. "It's a very *stylish* ridiculous budget."

He sighed and flipped it open. "You actually had this typed on Denwall letterhead?"

"I thought it gave it a certain weight."

Were his eyes bulging from his face? Because that's what it felt like. The bottom figure on the last page had him wondering if he'd have a coronary event before Father.

Bert closed the portfolio and slid it back to Zella.

"You barely even looked at it," she said.

"I looked enough." He sat back and removed his spectacles to wipe them with his handkerchief. "Sewn stitching?"

"If we're offering a book meant to grace tea tables and drawing rooms, it shouldn't fall apart after one reading. Sewn binding, not wire. I want women to keep these, not toss them out with old newspapers."

"Let me see if I have this straight." He began ticking off her list with his fingers. "You want exclusive European fashion house illustrations, fashion correspondents and illustrators assigned in various countries, and the best engravers and free-lance writers this side of the Atlantic?"

"Yes," she said evenly, not looking away from him for a second. "But I've also allocated for two of Denwall's in-house illustrators and three copywriters. The best ones."

He rubbed a hand over his face. "Zella, this is absurd. And what is the note by the printer's estimate? You haven't even received their quote yet?"

"You noticed."

"Of course I did. Well? What's the story?"

She hesitated and then gave him a wide grin, meant to charm and disarm. "I'll get them to you today. I promise."

"I hope their final numbers aren't too far off the ones they gave you when they were competing for Denwall's business."

"They won't be."

Bert pulled Zella's portfolio in front of him once more and perused her budget.

"You want Charles Dana Gibson for cover art?"

"If he isn't already contracted elsewhere."

He shot her a look. "He's booked out for a year, at least. Besides, he just got married in early November. He's on his honeymoon."

"How do you know that?"

Bert shrugged. "I went to his wedding." He flipped the page. "You're also budgeting for interior décor illustrations."

"As the board agreed."

She had him there.

He drummed his fingers against the edge of the desk. "You're awfully sure of yourself."

She smiled. "If I'm not, I can't expect anyone else to be."

Bert exhaled and flipped through more pages. "I'll approve some of the illustrators and freelance writers."

"I want all of them."

"You'll get half."

"Three-quarters."

"Zella—"

"You'll give me the full amount, eventually. You just need to pretend you fought harder."

He narrowed his eyes. "You are—"

"Stubborn? Yes, I've heard."

He rolled his eyes but couldn't quite keep the corner of his mouth from twitching. "If this project fails, we'll both be kicked out the door."

"It won't. People will fight to get their hands on their copy of a *Styles Book.*"

She sat back and beamed like she'd already won.

She was maddening.

Reluctantly, he reached into his desk and pulled out an invitation his mother had given to him for Zella. He slid the elegant, gold-embossed envelope across the desk. "From my mother."

Zella's eyebrows shot up. "What's this?"

"Of all things, an invitation to a debutante tea for my sister Caroline and Alexandra Dennison next week."

"Really? I can't say I've ever had the pleasure of attending a debutante function as a guest and not a lady correspondent." She pulled out the notecard and, for a few seconds, said nothing. She lifted her chin. Her eyes, gray like the sky on a stormy winter's day, glistened.

Tears?

Bert hadn't believed Zella had a sentimental bone in her body. "You've never been a guest at a debutante tea? Not even your own?" As soon as the words passed his lips, he could have kicked himself. Hard. Will had told him a little about Zella's upbringing. Ohio farm girls probably didn't have debutante seasons.

Zella threw back her head and laughed. The sound was

nothing like the tinkling laugh of society misses—the giggles that grated on his nerves.

"What's so funny?" he asked.

"Me as a debutante." She wiped a finger under her eye, effectively stopping the tear from rolling down her face.

Tears of mirth, he hoped.

"Even if my parents could have afforded a season, my father would never have spent his hard-earned money on the frivolities of a young woman. Besides, I left home the day I turned eighteen, two months before the season began." She chuckled once more and shook her head.

At least he'd managed to push the conversation past the awkward moment of the invitation. It was on the tip of his tongue to ask why she'd left home so young, but it really wasn't any of his business, and she stood before he had a chance to get the question out.

"I'll send your mother a note with my acceptance."

Watching her return to the elevator, Bert wondered if his mother knew what she was doing by inviting the sometimes outrageous Mrs. Capp.

Eight

Zella glanced at her desk calendar as she gathered her things. She slid her notebook into her reticule and buttoned her fitted coat.

Miss Leighton waved as Zella passed her desk on the way out of the publications department door. "Have a nice time."

Zella gave her a polite nod, but cringed at how the woman's words came across.

This wasn't a social call on company time, and she'd told Miss Leighton that several days ago when Helena Dennison extended the invitation.

The monthly meeting of the Women's Co-operative Association would be an excellent place to scout talent for the *Styles Book*. Helena, who helped manage the group even though she wasn't a woman of trade herself, had assured her there would be several promising women at the meeting—an illustrator trained in Paris, a writer recently returned from Vienna, and a milliner's apprentice whose fashion sketches had caught the eye of a magazine editor in Boston.

Zella didn't want to poach. Not outright. But Denwall's

book needed fresh voices. Preferably female talent who had an eye for beauty and trends.

If it weren't so cold, she would have walked the ten minutes to the New Century Club building. But, alas, the icy wind made walking that far a life-threatening venture.

As the streetcar rattled toward the city's center, Zella reviewed her mental checklist. She would introduce herself as a magazine editor and ask about portfolios and samples of writing. She couldn't mention the *Styles Book* outright, as she didn't want to give away the ideas for the publication in a public forum where competitors might be listening.

And under no circumstances would she linger. She had a pile of work waiting in her office, as well as a late-afternoon meeting with the in-house illustrators and a few freelance illustrators from New York to review their concept drawings.

Zella stepped off the car with ten minutes to spare and walked briskly toward The Club House, as the organization members dubbed the four-story building. She tipped her head back to peer at the well-designed architecture. Pompeiian brick and Indiana limestone, if she wasn't mistaken, which she rarely was in such matters. She'd read that the planning director and primary architect of the five-year-old structure were both women.

Inside, a few people were taking tea in a first-floor parlor, but other than that, the building seemed eerily quiet. She scanned the piece of paper she'd slipped into her reticule and took the stairs to the upper floor. Helena had told her The New Century Drawing Room could seat up to six hundred, but when she opened the door to the large hall, she was greeted not with the chatter of hundreds of women—or even ten, for that matter—but silence.

The meeting room stood mostly empty, except for a man at the far end who was sweeping the floor.

"Excuse me," she called. "Is this where the Women's Co-operative Association meeting is being held?"

He stopped and leaned on the broom handle. "Was. Ended around eleven-thirty."

"Ended?" Her heart sank to her shoes. "But the meeting was at noon."

The man peered at her over the top of his spectacles. "Not unless they had another meeting I don't know about. This one started at ten sharp."

"I must have misread the invitation," she murmured, though the words tasted wrong in her mouth.

The man tipped his head politely and went back to sweeping.

Zella stayed for a moment longer before turning away, closing the door softly behind her. She took the steps downstairs much more slowly than she'd taken them up.

How could I have gotten the time so wrong? She *didn't* get things wrong. She checked and rechecked everything. Normally. But her life hadn't been so normal lately, and she'd been moving at breakneck speed.

Still, that wasn't a good excuse.

Her stomach clenched at the thought that not only had she missed a golden opportunity to meet possible talent for the *Styles Book*, but she'd most likely disappointed Helena as well.

The street outside bustled with activity, and the scene blurred as her mind whirled. If she could, she'd kick herself. If anyone had failed to show up for one of her meetings, she wouldn't have offered much sympathy. She pulled her coat tighter and walked toward the Denwall offices. The cold that seeped through her clothes and boots was no less than she deserved.

Back at Denwall, she took the elevator down to the publications department. The hallway was quiet except for the soft hum of conversation in the corridor. She reached for the doorknob of her office door and stepped inside, moving directly to her desk. The calendar still lay open. *Thursday, December 11, 12:00, The New Century Drawing Room.* Why did it say twelve o'clock if it was ten?

Zella stared at the time. What had made her think the meeting was at twelve o'clock? She crossed the room to her filing cabinet, pulled open the middle drawer, and retrieved the correspondence folder.

Inside, tucked between the notes for a fashion feature and a clipped article on *Godey's*, was the letter Helena had forwarded last week. The original invitation to the committee meeting.

She unfolded it.

Thursday, December 11, 10:00 a.m.

Not twelve.

She sat down heavily in her chair.

The error was hers.

Now she'd have to apologize profusely to the Women's Co-op and then try to track down the women she'd hoped to speak with at the meeting.

Lucky for her, she'd likely be seeing Helena at the debutante tea for Caroline and Alexandra on Friday. Maybe she'd be kind enough to recreate a list of names for her.

Zella hated groveling.

Arriving at four o'clock sharp, as directed by the invitation to the debutante tea, Zella was met at the door of the Walraven mansion by the receiving line. In the line were the beaming hostesses, Laura Walraven and Myra Dennison, followed by Caroline and Alexandra, and almost every young woman coming out in Philadelphia high society that season.

Zella didn't attempt to commit all their names to memory.

The debutante tea, the first of many events hosted in honor of a daughter's coming out, was a fluttering sea of wealthy young women, all bright-eyed and brimming with optimism, their white gloves pristine, and their giggles headache-inducing.

By four-fifteen, the house was already overflowing with lace, pearls, and eager conversation, the air filled with the scent of freshly cut flowers, lavender sachets, and the faint, sugary aroma of petit fours. Laura commanded the gathering like a general commanding an army, directing the caterers and household staff so that everything ran smoothly. The woman was a wonder.

Having nothing else to do while the guests continued to arrive, Zella headed for the refreshment table.

Across the room, Helena waved, excused herself from the group of young women surrounding her, and headed Zella's way. She appeared effortlessly composed, the kind of woman who managed to be both timeless and entirely in step with the latest issue of *Harper's Bazaar*.

Her gown was a soft dove-gray silk faille, understated compared to the pastel confections worn by the debutantes, but far from plain. The bodice was close-fitted, with a high collar trimmed in white netting and pearl buttons. The gigot sleeves swelled at the shoulders and tapered gracefully to her gloved wrists, the fullness balanced by the smooth lines of her skirt.

A narrow velvet sash, almost the color of ink, encircled her waist, drawing the eye to Helena's enviable posture. No bustle —just a slight sweep to the back of the skirt, enough to rustle with intention as she moved. A jet brooch at her throat— likely heirloom, if Zella had to guess—was the only visible jewelry.

Zella took it all in with practiced efficiency. No frills, no lace, no overt attempt to compete with the youth around her. Helena didn't need to. Her style said exactly what it intended: *I've already done my season. I'm here to supervise yours.*

"Hello, Mrs. Capp."

Zella squared her shoulders. *Let the groveling commence.*

"First, I thought we agreed you'd call me Zella. Second, my sincerest apologies for mixing up the time of the meeting you invited me to."

Helena inclined her head, and her lips turned up. "First, I received your note. There's no need to apologize. These things happen. Second, feel free to call me Lena. The only person who still calls me Helena is Myra. She believes it's more refined. Oh, and call my sisters by their nicknames or they might not respond." She pulled an empty cup from the back of the table. "May I pour you some tea?"

Zella startled. How unlike a woman of high society to offer to serve someone below her station. "That would be lovely, thank you."

"Milk and sugar? Although you seem like the straight-tea kind of woman."

"Really? Well, actually, I'm a heavy-on-the-milk-and-sugar kind of girl."

"Bravo! As am I—when Myra's not looking."

"Worried about your figure, is she?"

Lena chortled and bobbed her head. "Always. I can't catch an eligible man if I'm portly. Or so my stepmother laments."

"Do you want to catch an eligible man?"

"No, I can't say that I do."

In that moment, Zella knew they would be fast friends.

She followed Lena to a settee on the far side of the room, away from the chatter of the debutantes. They both looked around the room and shook their heads.

"I feel old," Zella muttered.

Lena let out a quiet laugh, her blue eyes twinkling as she

surveyed the room. She lifted her teacup in mock salute. "I believe we're the elder stateswomen of the evening. But I'm only the elder and dutiful older sister. At least you are intriguing."

"Me?" She'd never thought of herself that way. Stubborn, yes. A bit outlandish by normal standards. But never something as delicious as *intriguing*.

"I can guarantee at least half these girls are wondering if you're secretly tragic or terribly scandalous."

Zella smirked. "Why choose? I can be both."

Across the room, Myra was in her element, floating from guest to guest, exuding gracious enthusiasm. Zella could already see her occasionally whispering in Alix's ear, likely reminding her to keep her shoulders back. Poor girl.

Alix's smile was bright, if a little shaky. She was arm in arm with Caroline, who was doing her best not to tower over every young man who stopped by to pay their respects. If she wasn't careful, she'd have stooped shoulders before she was twenty-five.

Zella had to admire the determination of debutantes. They endured an entire season of pushy mamas, carefully chosen words, and enough smiling to make one's cheeks ache.

She took another sip of her tea. "Do you remember being this age?"

Lena hummed in thought. "Barely. I was so focused on being a mother figure to my sisters that I didn't really have a season."

"Probably not the worst thing."

"Yes and no."

Before Zella could press further, Lena laid a hand on her forearm. "By the way, Myra asked me to extend an invitation. We'd be delighted if you joined us for church on Sunday. We attend St. Crispin's, as do a lot of other people you see here. But it's lovely. And they have a truly glorious soprano."

The offer caught Zella off guard. "That's kind of you."

"Don't feel obligated to come," Lena said lightly.

Zella wrestled with whether to accept or decline, and she shifted in her seat.

"Mrs. Capp. Miss Dennison."

Saved by the bell. Or by the man.

Zella glanced over her shoulder and found Bert standing there, looking out of place among the ruffles and ribbons.

She arched a brow. "Good afternoon, Mr. Walraven. I never imagined you at a debutante tea. Feeling social?"

"Not particularly," he muttered. "I didn't realize I'd be walking into this. Mother could have warned me that she'd invited every eighteen-year-old woman in the city."

Zella bit back a laugh. "It's a gathering of refined young women looking for good marriages. I thought that was precisely the sort of thing you Walravens approved of."

Bert shot her a pointed look but didn't rise to the bait.

Lena gestured to the empty seat beside them. "You might as well sit, Bert. Your mother's looking straight at you, so she knows you're here."

He exhaled and sat, though not without pulling at his collar, as if it had suddenly shrunk.

"Is Max here?" he asked.

"Looking for reinforcements?"

Bert gave Zella a sideways glance. "Absolutely. And I'm not ashamed to admit it."

Lena's eyes searched the filled-to-the-brim room. "My brother should be here soon. He promised Myra."

The conversation drifted after that, Lena shifting them toward harmless gossip about which debutante had the most eager suitors and whether Alix would survive Myra's matchmaking expectations.

Zella found herself genuinely enjoying the afternoon, despite her initial reluctance.

Finally, the parlor settled into a quieter hum. Laura's voice echoed faintly from the entry hall as she gave final farewells. Lena had disappeared to help Alix and Caroline with something upstairs.

Zella stood by the window, absently swirling the last of her tea. Outside, the shadows stretched longer across the Walraven lawn, and a warm golden light filtered through the lace curtains.

Bert moved to stand beside her, his hands tucked in his pockets. "You survived and did well."

"Your tone makes it sound like an insult."

His mouth lifted at one corner. "Let's just say I'm not enamored with society events."

They stood in silence for a few comfortable seconds.

"Did you see the printer's estimate I left on your desk?" After an hour of looking for the misplaced proposal, she'd finally found it at the back of a drawer she reserved for illustrations.

"I saw it. Glad it came in where you thought it would."

Alix and Lena strolled through the room, arm in arm, their heads together as Alix whispered something in Lena's ear.

"Lena invited me to church." Zella wasn't entirely sure why she blurted that piece of news to Bert. Most likely, he didn't care how she spent her Sundays.

"Lena tends to do that. Think of others. But I'm sure she'd genuinely like for you to come."

"She said it's at St. Crispin's."

"That's where my family attends every Sunday."

Zella tapped her finger against her chin. "Isn't that the one with the dome? The grand organ? Rows of carriages parked out front on Sundays?"

"That's the one."

She huffed. "I passed it last week on the way to the market.

Everyone streaming out like peacocks. Hats taller than infants."

Bert laughed around the petit four he'd just popped into his mouth. "You're not wrong."

It surprised her that he didn't try to defend the showiness.

"Some do come to be seen," he said. "Or for the gossip afterward. But not all. My mother's been going since she was a newlywed. Always sits in the second pew on the right. Brings the same old Bible every week, pages nearly falling out."

Zella considered that. "And the pastor?"

"He's good. Steady. Not flashy."

She said nothing, but he didn't seem to need her answer.

"You don't have to decide now," he added. "But if you come, don't sit too far in the back. From there, the view's all hat brims and feathers."

That coaxed a reluctant smile from her.

As he turned to go, he paused. "You know," he said over his shoulder, "you're not the only one who wrestles with faith."

And then he was gone.

Zella stood by the window a moment longer. She wasn't sure she wanted to show up on Sunday. But for the first time in a long while, she wasn't entirely sure she didn't.

NINE

Bert rarely fidgeted in church.

He came most Sundays, not out of habit exactly, and certainly not to impress anyone. It was one of the few places in his life that hadn't been claimed by Denwall, by duty, or by expectation.

His gaze drifted as the congregation rustled into stillness, the clatter of hymnals and the shuffle of coats subsiding. That's when he saw her.

Zella.

She slipped into the pew across the aisle, her movements composed. She wore a simple dove-gray dress, high-necked and unadorned, with only a narrow velvet ribbon at the collar and a modest hat that dipped just above one brow. No feathers. Not showy. And yet, he couldn't look away. Somehow, the absence of embellishment made her more striking than ever.

It wasn't just her beauty, with her ink-black hair, heart-shaped face, and wide gray eyes. Maybe it was more the way she moved. Understated confidence was the only way he could think to describe it. She moved through the world like she knew what she wanted and precisely how to get it.

Even surrounded by Philadelphia's churchgoing elite, she stood tall. All five feet three inches of her.

He admired that she made no apologies for her ambition. He, on the other hand, had spent years shrinking his aspirations down to something practical. Something manageable. Head of finance. Reliable. Invisible. Safe.

He hadn't wanted more than that, even if Father was disappointed in his "lack of ambition."

Will once told Bert that he envied him because he didn't take Father too seriously. Didn't let the man's calculated words affect him. Will said Bert knew who he was and was happy in his own skin.

Bert wasn't so sure.

The organ swelled, pulling him back as the congregation rose for the first hymn. He flipped the page automatically, but then he heard her. That voice. Low and clear, warm as sunlight through stained glass.

He'd heard it once before, at Ivy's church in New York. Zella sang without hesitation, her voice sure and steady, as if every lyric were a memory stitched to her soul. And she knew them all. Every word, obviously, because she never looked down at the hymnal. He watched her lips shape the verses of "Come Thou Fount of Every Blessing"—a hymn he half-mumbled his way through—and something in him tightened with envy.

Maybe not for her voice, or her memory for lyrics, but for whatever it was that gave her that confidence, even when she didn't seem to belong.

The congregation took their seats, and he sat with his family in their usual pew. Bert listened to the steady cadence of the pastor's voice as if it were any other Sunday.

But lately, he felt restless, like a boat adrift on a river.

He shifted slightly in his seat, rolling his shoulders, trying to push away the familiar, nagging tension that had settled there.

Ever since that morning in Madison Square Park, when he had been caught off guard, dragged to the ground, and beaten unconscious, a feeling of vulnerability had followed him like a shadow.

He hadn't seen it coming. Hadn't been able to stop it.

And worse than the pain, worse than the bruises and the humiliation, was the helplessness and the split-second realization that, for all his confidence, for all his athleticism and discipline, he was completely powerless.

So he had done what any reasonable man would do.

He took back control. Pushing himself at the boxing club and conditioning his mind and body so that if it ever happened again, he would be ready.

And yet, here he was, in a church, listening to a man at the pulpit talk about surrender.

"Come to me, all you who labor and are heavy laden, and I will give you rest. Take my yoke upon you and learn from me, for I am gentle and lowly in heart, and you will find rest for your souls. For my yoke is easy, and my burden is light."

The pastor paused, and his eyes shifted to take in the congregation before him.

"There are those among us today who know the weight of carrying burdens. Who have spent years relying on no one but themselves. Who have come to believe that control is the only way to survive."

Across the aisle, Zella shifted in her seat.

The pastor's voice rose. "You work, you plan, you guard your heart, because somewhere along the way, you learned that to depend on others is to risk being ruled, being hurt, being bound by something you never agreed to.

"And perhaps—if you are honest—you believe that to trust God is no different. That He is another master waiting to lay heavy burdens upon you. Another voice that demands you obey without question. Another authority who takes rather than gives.

"But Jesus says otherwise. He calls you to trust not in chains, but in freedom. He offers to take your burdens and worries from you."

The pastor closed his Bible. "The question is, will you accept the gift?"

Bert's fingers curled slightly against his knee.

Like he hinted to Zella yesterday at the debutante tea, he wrestled with faith. Not his faith in the existence of an Almighty but his faith in God's sovereign hand.

He'd cultivated a tight grip on control of his life.

And the last thing he wanted to do was let go.

†

Zella shifted in her seat. The words the pastor spoke of surrendering control shouldn't have struck her as hard as they did, but there it was, that quiet tug deep in her chest.

She hadn't planned to come this morning. Church wasn't something she avoided outright, but it lived at the edge of her life, like anything that required too much trust.

She'd said yes when the Dennisons asked, mainly because she couldn't think of a polite excuse. But now, sitting here in this sanctuary laced with evergreen garlands and candlelight, her breath caught when the pastor asked, "Will you accept the gift?"

Her spine stiffened.

She had simply done what needed to be done in her life. Taken control. Moved forward. Survived.

The scent of beeswax and pine hung thick in the air. Candles flickered on either side of the altar, and a shaft of winter light broke through the stained-glass windows overhead, casting jewel-toned pools across the aisle.

As the final hymn began, she stood with the rest of the congregation. Her gaze wandered, not out of distraction, but disquiet. Something about today had knocked her slightly askew.

And she caught sight of Bert across the aisle.

She'd known he was there because she'd passed him on the way to her seat. But she'd refused to look his way, even when she felt his eyes studying her profile.

During the closing hymn, she gave in to temptation and took a surreptitious peek.

He stood with his family, his large hands sharing a hymnal with his sister. His voice carried across the aisle, and she almost giggled. His voice was awful. It sounded like a bleating sheep on the high notes. When he looked up and saw her smiling at him, he shrugged and grinned. Not ashamed at all.

Zella appreciated his self-awareness coupled with confidence.

When the final notes faded and the congregation began to shuffle toward the doors, Zella lingered behind the Dennisons. She adjusted her gloves slowly, grateful for something to do with her hands. A few people nodded politely as they passed by.

She had just entered the vestibule when a voice beside her drew her back.

"I'm glad you came today, Zella."

Zella shifted to find Lena at her side.

"Thank you for inviting me."

Outside, the snow had let up, leaving a soft white dusting over the pavement, muffling the sounds of the surrounding city.

Reaching the line of carriages, they both watched as families gathered on the sidewalk. Mothers tugged on gloves, and fathers lifted children into their vehicles, the chatter warm despite the cold.

And there she stood—Zella Capp, spinster and widow-who-wasn't—on the periphery, both part of the scene and outside it.

"You know," Lena said suddenly, "spinsterhood isn't such a terrible fate."

Zella let out a quiet laugh. "Is that what you tell yourself?"

"I don't have to. I chose this." Lena's tone was matter-of-fact. "And I don't regret it."

Zella studied her, expecting to find a flicker of doubt, but there was none. Lena didn't carry the wistfulness Zella had come to expect in unmarried women of a certain age. There was no apology in her eyes.

"Most people think I should feel pitiful," Lena went on. "Especially after raising my siblings. But I like my life. I've had choices. And I still do."

"And you don't feel lonely?"

"Never."

A breeze caught the hem of Lena's coat and blew a strand of hair across her cheek. She didn't seem to notice.

There was something effortless about her, a kind of ease Zella rarely encountered, especially among women who'd chosen a life outside society's expectations.

"I think," Lena added, quieter now, "that solitude and loneliness aren't always the same thing. Some of us make peace with quiet. Others fear it."

Zella wanted to ask which one Lena was. But before she could, a familiar voice cut through the bustle around them.

"Hello again, ladies."

Bert stood just a few steps away, his hands tucked in his coat pockets, his breath clouding the cold air, and his expression unreadable behind his spectacles.

"Hello, Bert." Lena arched a brow and stepped back.

"Excuse me while I check on my sisters." Zella caught a flicker of amusement in the woman's retreat.

"I didn't think you'd come," Bert said.

"Neither did I."

He seemed like he wanted to say more, and his eyes lingered on her face. "You sing well."

Zella blinked. "Pardon?"

"I could hear you in there," he clarified. "You sing well."

"Thank you. And you sing with enthusiasm."

"Ah, yes. I've been asked several times to join the church choir."

Zella enjoyed Bert's quick wit. "I'm sure you have."

Lena called her name as their carriage rolled up. Zella had been invited to join the Dennisons for lunch.

"Well, I'll see you tomorrow at work, I assume," Zella said to Bert.

"I'd like to see your final budget this week, Zella. With all the adjustments we discussed. Don't forget."

She waved and dashed off, not giving him time to ask for her agreement, and vowing not to be caught unawares next time.

TEN

The publications department's radiator clicked, and the grandfather clock in the corner of the room chimed six. Zella slipped into her office and took a deep breath.

The weekly management meeting had run long, as they always did when one or another insisted on picking apart every suggestion. Zella had smiled through it, taken her notes, and waited until the last man rose from the conference table before retreating to her office.

She loosened the collar of her blouse and unfastened her cuffs as she walked. Outside, the halls had grown quiet, the energy of the building ebbing with the early winter dusk. She passed the mail clerk wheeling away an empty basket and nodded at the janitor who tipped his cap.

Zella had learned to love the stillness of late afternoons in the Denwall offices, when most employees had gone for the day and the corridors lost their bustle. It was when she did her best thinking. Her clearest planning.

She pulled open her desk drawer to retrieve the final marked proofs she planned to read through before tomorrow's board review. An envelope, unmarked and unopened, sat on top of the stack.

Frowning, she picked it up and slid her mother-of-pearl letter opener under the flap. She pulled out a folded sheet of paper that was heavier than a typical memo slip. Unlike most interoffice notes, which were often handwritten in hurried fashion, this one was typed.

Not signed. No initials. No sender name. Sharp words, three sentences long.

> You are not good enough for this job, and soon that will come to light. I advise you to pack your bags and go back to New York. You're not wanted here.

Her breath caught, and a faint ringing started in her ears. It was the same feeling she'd had once, years ago, when her father tore up her story pages and said no man worth anything wanted a wife who thought herself clever.

She'd worked too hard to let the anonymous venom undo her.

And yet they knew exactly where to strike.

Not good enough.

She bit her lower lip and set the paper down, as if letting go would ease the tremble in her fingertips. But the feeling of worthlessness clung to her—in the pit of her stomach, in the corners of her thoughts, curling like smoke.

Hadn't that fear always hovered behind her every success?

Zella sat back slowly. This wasn't a joke. It was meant to wound without leaving fingerprints.

For a moment, all the air in the room felt thick. The radiator hissed. And in her chest, the old, cold ache she thought she'd buried began to stir again.

Not good enough.

The words burrowed like tiny barbs.

She swallowed hard. Who could have sent the message?

Bert's image came to mind, and she immediately dismissed it. He was far too honorable to stoop so low. Perhaps one of the executives who didn't like her budget requests? An illustrator or freelance writer who wasn't picked for the *Styles Book*? Or someone in the production department right outside her office door?

She thought of Sylvia Leighton, who was so polished, helpful, and complimentary, but also strangely evasive, and too poised.

No, that didn't sit right. Miss Leighton had flaws, but she'd been nothing but cordial. This letter was petty and mean-spirited.

Zella folded the note and slipped it into the bottom drawer of her desk.

She pushed up from her chair and paced the small confines of her office, one hand pressed to her middle. It shouldn't hurt so much. Not after everything she'd proven. Not after all the work.

She wished for a trusted friend here. Someone like Ivy or Florence.

Florence.

If only she could leave Philadelphia behind for a few days to visit the dear woman who always knew the right things to say. She might not be able to now, but she could in April.

Zella returned to her desk and took a deep breath.

She debated whether another letter to Florence would seem overzealous. But what if the one she'd written when she first moved to Philadelphia had never reached Chicago? What if something was terribly wrong, and Florence hadn't been able to write back?

Zella steadied her hand and dipped her pen in the inkwell.

The letter began with the standard greeting and comment about the weather, but she quickly moved to inquire about Florence's health and whether she was up to receiving a visitor in the spring.

> *The last few weeks have been a whirlwind, but you are on my mind often. If you are busy and haven't found the time to write, I understand completely. Or if my coming to see you in April is a burden, I understand that as well. I only ask that you let me know.*
>
> *Wishing you peace and strength this Christmas.*
>
> *Yours with warm regards,*
> *Zella*

She added a Christmas card decorated with a gold-etched border and a snowy church scene and sealed the envelope.

Dare she say a prayer? Were the thoughts that ran through her mind, hoping Florence was well, the same thing?

Zella stood and took her cloak from the hook by the door. Instead of placing the letter in her outgoing mail basket, she decided she would deliver it to the post office herself.

Besides, she needed the fresh air.

Bert didn't relish going out in a snowstorm, but it was only a week until Christmas, and his mother had requested that he spend most of Christmas week at the family home in Rittenhouse Square, rather than at his house on Lotus Street.

She wanted her family around her for the coming festivities. She'd insisted. Will was even coming in from New York at the end of the week and bringing Ivy and her grandmother with him.

None of the Walraven offspring could refuse their mother.

The snow was falling in thick, blinding sheets when Bert arrived, and the entire front walkway was already buried under several inches of white. He'd barely alighted the carriage when he spotted his mother and Caroline, their cloaks whipped by the wind, halfway up the walk and clearly struggling to gain a secure footing. And before he could call out to be careful or wait for a footman to assist them, Mother slipped.

Bert was down the path in seconds.

By the time he reached them, Caroline was kneeling on the icy walkway, her hat askew, cheeks flushed, and panic in her eyes.

"I told her to wait."

"I think I've hurt my leg. And maybe my wrist," Mother said, her voice tight. "Bert, help me up, please."

Instead of pulling her to her feet, he bent and picked her up. He turned toward the house, his mother in his arms.

"Caroline, please tell one of the footmen to fetch Dr. Rawlins. And find Father."

Mother shook her head. "I don't think I need a doctor." But she grimaced in pain.

"I'll go find a footman," Caroline said.

Smart girl.

Within two hours, Dr. Rawlins had arrived at the house and examined Mother. Father asked rapid-fire questions of the kind physician as the family gathered at Mother's bedside.

"Mrs. Walraven has suffered two injuries from the fall, though, mercifully neither appears to be life-threatening. The wrist is a clean fracture of the distal radius. Quite common when one falls and attempts to catch oneself. The bone is properly aligned, and with care, it should heal well. The greater concern is the knee. The joint is swollen and tender, and I believe there's damage to one or more of the inner ligaments."

Father pushed a hand through his thick black hair. "Will she be able to walk?"

"I recommend bed rest for the first week, followed by limited movement in a wheeled seat for possibly another six weeks. Even after that, she must take care. A misstep too soon, and she risks lasting instability. But yes, she will be able to walk eventually."

He turned to Mother, who sat propped up in her bed while the rest of the family sat in various places around the bedroom, except for Father, who stood by the bed and held Mother's hand.

"You've been fortunate, Madam," Dr. Rawlins said. "But healing will require patience. Let others help you."

Once the doctor had left, Father asked the housekeeper to have Cook prepare dinner to be served at Mother's bedside—although Mother grumbled that it wasn't necessary that they all eat with her.

"I still can't believe I fell," she said in a wobbly voice. "And right before Christmas, and *evreefing*. Caro's ... what's its name?" The laudanum was beginning to take effect, praise the Lord. Bert hated seeing his mother in pain.

"The staff can handle all the Christmas preparations, dear, and we can hire someone to assist with Caroline's debutante events," Father said. "You'll still direct the planning."

Mother gave him a withering look. "Don't be *diculous*. We can't hire someone. There's *ceptions*, dinners, and a ball." Her eyes fluttered closed.

There was a beat of silence, broken only by the popping of a log in the hearth.

Caroline, seated on the rug with one of her two Pomeranians in her lap, sighed. "I don't need to have a debutante season, and I don't want Mother to worry."

"Your mother will be very disappointed if you don't follow through with your plans."

"I'll help you, Caro," Ned offered.

The surprise on Caroline's face was almost comical.

Bert cleared his throat. "I think hiring someone is a good idea. Myra will offer to help, but she already has enough on her hands just dealing with Alix's debut. Since we have no female relatives who can assist, aside from Grandmother Shaw, we have little choice."

"No! Not Grandmother!" Caroline said, jumping to her feet and knocking Lily off her lap. "I mean, I love her dearly, but she'd ruin everything. I'd end up dressed like a relic from the seventies." She whirled toward Father. "I have an idea! What about Mrs. Capp? She knows all the latest fashions and has written a slew of articles on debutante affairs."

Father's brow furrowed. "Mrs. Capp? I don't know ..."

"That's a brilliant idea, Caro." Ned slapped his knee. "She's clever, stylish, and unflappable. And we all like her."

"She's also not a Walraven, or a Dennison for that matter, and not part of our circle," Father said matter-of-factly. "What would she know about planning a proper debut?" He glanced at Mother, who was sound asleep.

Caroline frowned. "She has better taste than half the ladies who *are* in our circle."

"Which is exactly why it'll put the matrons' noses out of joint," Ned said from the window seat, where he was eating biscuits straight from the tin. "Sounds like a lark. I say do it."

"This is not a game, Edward." Father scowled at his youngest son.

Standing near the fireplace, his arms crossed, Bert watched the conversation unfold. Part of him agreed with Father. Zella wasn't the right person to help or guide Caroline. He doubted she'd have the patience for all the season entailed—most of it fluff and nonsense.

And Caroline, for all her poise, was still young. Impressionable. Would Mother really want someone as bold and independent as Zella influencing her?

Caroline folded her hands in a prayer-like plea. "Please, ask Mrs. Capp to help me. Alix will be positively giddy. She adores her."

Everyone in the family had a difficult time denying the only Walraven daughter anything.

And—blast it—Ned wasn't entirely wrong. The idea of Philadelphia society having to endure someone from outside their ranks at every debutante event was almost appealing. There'd be ruffled feathers aplenty.

Still—

"She's great at what she does," Bert said slowly. "But that doesn't mean she's the best person to guide Caroline through planning events for the season or attending events with her."

"Why not?" Caroline asked, brows rising. "You said yourself she was sharp. You've been working with her for weeks."

"That's different."

Ned sat up from his slouched position. "Besides her obvious knowledge about fashion and society events, Mrs. Capp can more than hold her own. She'll protect Caro from the other mamas of debutantes." Ned shuddered. "They can be a vicious lot."

"If you all want me to have my debut this season so as not to disappoint Mother, we have little choice. Assuming Mrs. Capp even agrees." Caroline paused and tapped a finger to her chin. "Maybe I can offer to pay her for her trouble. I have pin money saved up."

Father sighed. "You don't need to use your pin money, Caroline. I'll offer to pay Mrs. Capp."

Bert supposed it was their best option.

But an irritating voice in the back of his head wondered just how Zella herself would respond to this idea.

With amusement? With horror?

Or would she take it as a challenge?

He wasn't so eager to find out.

ELEVEN

Laura Walraven thanked the Lord for small mercies. Although it had been a full day since she'd fallen, the family had hovered around her like a bunch of mother hens until about fifteen minutes earlier, and her bedroom was finally quiet.

Charles had retreated to his study, muttering about correspondence. Caroline had gone over to the Dennisons to tell them the news about the accident, and Ned wandered off in search of biscuits. If only her eldest son would do the same.

Instead, Bert remained, leaning against the mantel with that familiar guarded posture. The snow still pressed against the windows, muting the city's noise and wrapping the house in a hush except for the pop of the well-lit fire.

Laura shifted carefully, adjusting the pillows beneath her sling with her good hand. "You're brooding," she said.

"I'm standing."

She arched a brow.

Bert smiled faintly but didn't move. "You should be resting."

"I am. I've been resting for two days."

"It's just over twenty-four hours. And you shouldn't be

worrying, which I can tell you are by the crease between your brows."

"I'm supposed to worry. It's what mothers do."

"And you do it well," Bert said with a nod.

She gave a soft snort of amusement, then studied him a moment. If he was going to hover over her, she might as well take advantage of the moment alone with him. "Are you all right, dear? You seem preoccupied."

"I'm fine, Mother." He looked away, jaw tightening.

"No, you're not. You haven't been for some time."

Laura waited for a reply, but none came, and Bert's shoulders stiffened. She chose her next words carefully. "You carry your silence like a shield. But I'm your mother, and I know when you're hiding something."

Bert stared into the fire.

"I want more for you than ledgers and duty," she continued, her voice softer now. "You've been working beside your father since you were barely out of university. There's more to life than Denwall."

He shrugged. "I don't have a problem with my life. There's nothing wrong with stability."

"No," she agreed. "But there's something wrong with believing that's all you're allowed."

She sighed when he didn't comment. "You're a good man, Bert. Steady, loyal, principled. But you are not only a set of responsibilities. You're a son. A brother. A man with a mind of his own and a heart, whether you like it or not."

When he finally spoke, his voice was quiet. "I know what you're thinking. You want me to fall in love."

"I want you to *live*," she said. "And yes, to love, God willing. I know not everyone marries. But I've watched you shrink from it, not because you don't want it, but because you're afraid."

He stiffened again, the firelight flickering across his profile. "It's not fear."

"No?" she asked but strove to keep any sharpness from her voice. "I think you've had someone watching over every move you've made your entire life pushing you to be who he wants you to be. That's made you a cautious person in your other relationships."

His gaze shot to hers, surprise on his face. "What do you mean?"

"I know how difficult your father can be. Ambition is ingrained in him, and he wants his sons to be that way as well. His focus is on Denwall, and always has been. I know his faults, believe me. But he is a good man. Faithful to me, and although he doesn't show it well, he loves you and all his children."

"I know he does. I've learned to live with his disappointment in my lack of desire to be at the helm of Denwall. But what does that have to do with me avoiding marriage?"

"You think you've had enough pressure from someone with great expectations. You don't want a wife who will do the same thing."

Bert chuckled. "That's very insightful of you, Mother. I've never actually thought of my reluctance to marry in quite that way. But you could be right. Women in our world are very demanding. Present company excluded, of course."

"Of course." She gave him a small smile. "I don't think you're completely misguided. Society women can be shallow and self-centered. But not all eligible women are from our world."

"Don't let Father hear you say that."

"I can handle your father." She had for thirty-three years. "Just look at Will. He's marrying someone who isn't from Philadelphia society, but she is perfect for him. Your father sees it, too, even if he's reluctant to admit it."

Should she let him ponder on that or should she push the thought that had weighed on her heart for almost a month?

Hang it. She was his mother. She'd push.

"Mrs. Capp is a lovely woman. She's about your age, isn't she?" she asked lightly.

He gave a soft huff, more disbelief than humor. "She's one or two years older, I believe." He pointed a finger at her. "But don't think I don't know what you're up to. Zella's the last woman in Philadelphia I'd choose."

She begged to differ. "Exactly."

That made him laugh, the sound low and surprised.

"If she accepts our proposition to help with Caroline's debut, you'll see her even more than you do now."

"She's not going to accept Father's money."

"Well then, hopefully she'll want to do it anyway. That's an opportunity for you worth seizing."

"She's a whirlwind," he said.

"She's a woman who knows what she wants and doesn't apologize for it." Laura paused and tilted her head. "You've always admired that in others."

He turned back toward the fire, the humor fading into something thoughtful.

"I'm not saying she's the one," she said quickly. "I'm just saying she might be good for you. Sometimes the thing we think is safest is simply the thing we can control. But love involves risk."

Bert said nothing, but his expression shifted. Just slightly.

Laura leaned her head back against the cushions, suddenly exhausted. The pain in her knee throbbed, dull but persistent, and she closed her eyes.

After a moment, she felt movement. Bert was adjusting her shawl, gently tucking it around her shoulders like he had when he was twelve and she'd fallen asleep with a book in her lap on the parlor settee.

She opened one eye. "You're a good son, Bert."

"You're a maddening mother."

"Yes, well," she murmured, smiling, "the best ones are."

He lingered a moment longer, then straightened. "I'll have Cook bring you some tea."

"Don't think I didn't see you dodge the rest of this conversation."

"I'm just postponing it."

Her lips twitched. "Wise man."

And as he left the room, she watched him go with the same silent prayer she'd whispered for years.

Lord, please let him find what he's looking for—even if he doesn't know he's searching.

＊

The streets outside still bore the remnants of the storm— slushy and gray, the kind of snow that dirtied hems and made everyone a little grumpier than usual. But inside the publications department, the air was warm, humming with the usual murmur of low voices, typewriters, and brisk footsteps.

Zella sat at her desk, reviewing in-house illustration samples for the home décor section—a study in French Gothic parlor design that would dazzle anyone with a fireplace large enough to warrant carved angels flanking it.

She thought she'd also received the first in-house illustrations of the jewelry layout. She rifled through the papers on her desk and in her drawers. Normally an organized person, the aggressive timetable on this project made her feel a little scatterbrained.

A knock sounded at her door.

"Come in," she called.

Bert stepped in, holding a small envelope in his hand.

"Good morning." His tone was a tad grumpy. Funny, she'd always assumed he was a morning person, since he used to get up early to walk to the park when he lived in New York. Of course, that was before the mugging.

"Good morning." She arched a brow. "No snide comment to start the day?"

"I'm pacing myself." He crossed the room and placed the envelope on her desk. "From my mother. She asked me to deliver it personally."

"Your mother? Another debutante invitation?" Zella couldn't imagine going to another tea.

"She slipped on some ice on Friday."

"Oh, dear! Is she all right?" Zella truly liked Laura Walraven and hoped she wasn't injured.

"She's hurt her wrist and knee badly enough that she's been ordered to rest for six weeks. Now she's trying to figure out how to manage everything with Christmas five days away and Caroline's debutante season in full swing."

Zella broke the envelope's seal and pulled out the note. The handwriting was elegant, as a society lady's penmanship should be.

> *My dear Mrs. Capp,*
> *In light of my unfortunate injuries and the pressing demands of Caroline's debut, I find myself in need of capable assistance. Caroline—quite enthusiastically, I must say—suggested you, and I am inclined to agree.*
> *There are a number of events to prepare for, as well as others that Caroline must attend with a proper chaperone. I hesitate to impose, but the notion occurred to me that this might prove a*

worthy subject for the European Styles Book. You mentioned, I believe, the possibility of including an entire section devoted to the debutante.

Please do not feel obliged to accept what may seem an egregious request, but I should be most grateful if you would consider it.

Warmly,

Laura Walraven

Zella stared at the letter a moment longer than necessary, her heart skipping once, then settling back into its usual guarded rhythm.

"Is your mother taking laudanum for the pain? I understand it can cause delirium," she said, folding the letter carefully.

"Nope," Bert said, sliding his hands into his trouser pockets. "She wrote this in a fully cognitive state. And Father would like to pay you for your time."

"That's not necessary." Zella waved a dismissive hand. "Assuming I accept," she added quickly. "I'm flattered that they'd think of me. I *have* written a dozen articles on what a debutante should say, wear, and eat for breakfast, but as I told you, I've never actually experienced a debutante season firsthand. I would think that would disqualify me as an acceptable stand-in for your mother."

When he didn't respond, she released a self-deprecating chuckle. "And frankly, I'm not sure the other society mamas would approve. I've been told I can be quite outrageous."

"I agree. I tried to convince my mother that this might not be a sound plan."

Zella wasn't sure whether to laugh at the seriousness on Bert's face or be offended at his blunt remark.

Before she could respond, he lifted a finger. "However, you're the person Caroline and my mother feel most comfortable with." He shrugged his broad shoulders. "Besides, it will save you from having to hire a reporter to write about the season's activities."

"Your father won't like it."

Bert let out a quiet laugh. "He already doesn't."

Zella smiled, just a little. "Then maybe I should say yes, just to irritate him."

"I knew you were a troublemaker," Bert said, grinning now.

She scanned the note again, tracing the edge with her thumb.

Something about Laura's words tugged at her. Not just the formality or the flattery—but the assumption that Zella had something to offer beyond managing the *Styles Book*.

That she could guide a young woman through the most watched, most whispered-about season of her life.

Zella set the note down and lifted her chin. "When do you need my answer?"

"My mother and Caroline will be anxious, and that will spoil the holiday festivities." Bert studied her for a beat. "I'd appreciate it if you could give me an answer by the end of the day."

"I'll think about it and let you know tomorrow night." Did he realize she'd be at his parents' house then?

He gave her a crooked grin. "That's Christmas Eve. I'd like your answer by messenger tomorrow morning."

"Surely you realize there's a lot to consider. I have a full plate as it is." Zella gestured toward the wire baskets overflowing on her desk. "If I say yes, this job won't have my full attention." She raised an eyebrow and waited while he digested the hint. He was over a barrel, and he knew it.

"Let's hear it, Zella. What do you want?"

"I'm working with a fabulous freelance copywriter out of New York, but she has other clients. I want to hire her full time, so her focus is solely on the *Styles Book*, until the end of March."

Bert pushed his spectacles up his nose, his lips quirking. "We'll write up a contract to retain her exclusively for the next four weeks. Take it or leave it."

In that moment, Zella realized he'd *expected* her to negotiate and had relished the challenge.

She knew a good opponent when she saw one. And Bert, infuriatingly, made every round feel like a draw.

TWELVE

Despite her rocky upbringing, one of Zella's favorite times of the year as a young child was Christmas Eve.

Even now, she could recall the scent of pine sap on her mittens as she and Rosina waited at the edge of the woods for their father to emerge, scowling beneath his fur cap, with a crooked spruce slung over his shoulder. Mam would be waiting with mulled cider and a tin of cinnamon biscuits, pretending not to mind the bits of bark and snow they tracked through the parlor.

Rosina always insisted on trimming the very top branch herself, even if it meant dragging over the piano bench and wobbling with theatrical flair until Mam shrieked in alarm. Afterward, they'd sit cross-legged by the fire, threading popcorn and cranberries, while Mam hummed "God Rest Ye Merry, Gentlemen" and stitched last-minute gifts by lamplight.

That was how it was until Rosina married and left for New York, leaving Zella behind on the farm with their melancholy mother and a father whose bitterness deepened with every season. The tree still went up each year, but no one sang by the fire or strung popcorn. Year after year, Christmas Eve became even quieter and more austere.

Now that Zella had Ivy and Jemima to spend the holiday with, Christmas Eve was once again a lovely experience. Through Rosina, Ivy carried on the same traditions, except that the tree was purchased from a local tree seller.

This year, Zella had planned to take the train to New York early on Christmas Eve morning and spend the following two days with the Kings in their apartment above the bookshop. At the last minute, however, she, Ivy, and Jemima received an invitation to join Will and the Walraven family in Philadelphia.

So, at noon on the holiest of days, dressed in her prettiest visiting toilette and holding a bag of carefully wrapped gifts, Zella stepped into the carriage sent to bring her to Rittenhouse Square. Laura had insisted she spend the night, so she handed the driver her overnight case to attach to the back of the vehicle.

Inside the Walraven townhouse, Zella handed the butler her cloak and turned in a circle to take in the loveliness of the foyer, which was cheerfully adorned with holly and ivy, red ribbon, and sprigs of mistletoe tucked in the chandeliers.

Two Pomeranians—one all black in coloring, and the other all white—came racing down the hallway, past a laughing Caroline, and straight toward Zella. They skidded to a halt at her feet, and like two little soldiers, both sat and peered up through a fluff of fur. She bent and gave them each a rub behind the ears.

"Mother's in the parlor," Caroline said. "The Dennisons are here for a short visit."

"So I gather." Zella could hear the chatter of voices down the hall. "Who are these two angels?"

Caroline giggled. "More like two little devils. The white one is Lily, the older, and the black one is Lucy."

"Are they your dogs?" Zella couldn't imagine Will, Bert, or Ned for that matter, claiming these two fluff balls as their own.

"Mother and Father gave Lily to me for my fourteenth birthday and Lucy for my sixteenth."

Zella followed Caroline down the hall and through the parlor door. Laura sat in a wicker wheelchair with one leg propped up and her injured arm in a sling. Myra was in a Chippendale chair next to Laura. Lena, Lou, and Tris sat on one settee while Alix sat on the other.

Alix patted the seat beside her. "Come sit between Caro and me, Mrs. Capp."

Caroline beamed. "Oh, yes, please do!"

"Give her a moment to catch her breath, girls," Laura said. "It's good to see you, Zella."

"And you. I was so sorry to hear about your fall. I hope you're not in too much pain."

"Not much. And thank you for the kind note accepting my very pushy request to help us with Caroline's debut."

Zella smiled and took the seat between the two debutantes. "It sounds like a ball. Pardon the pun."

"Will, Ivy, and Mrs. King will be here in a few hours. Something came up at the New York store, and Will telephoned that they'd be a little late."

"I'm looking forward to seeing them." That was an understatement. She hadn't seen Ivy or Jemima since the engagement dinner six weeks ago.

Zella had tossed and turned the night before, wondering whether she should use this time together to tell Ivy about the lie she'd perpetrated for almost thirteen years, but thought better of it. No sense ruining everyone's Christmas. She'd write Ivy in the new year and explain everything.

Yes, she was a coward.

"May I pour you a cup of tea?" Myra asked.

"That would be lovely."

And it was.

The next twenty minutes flew by as they discussed the coming events of the social season, including the Charity Ball at the Academy of Music. According to Myra, it was one of the most popular events of the year and would be the first time that the season's debutantes danced in public.

Myra set her teacup on a side table. "Laura and I are both on the organizing committee and have been for the last three years. However, it's too much for her this year, and Charles has requested she sit this one out. So the committee met on Tuesday and voted to ask you to take her place this season."

"You've already voted?" Surprise at the boldness coursed through Zella.

Myra gave a rueful smile. "We did. Not unanimously, but firmly enough."

"I suppose you need someone organized, unsentimental, and who can say no when called for?"

"Exactly," Myra said, without a hint of shame.

Zella accepted the slice of cranberry cake that Lena pressed into her hand.

"I apologize for the ambush," Lena said. "You can say no."

"Helena's on the committee too," Myra said, completely ignoring Lena's remark. "Proceeds from this year's ball will go to the University of Pennsylvania Student Aid Fund, the Southeastern Hospital for Women and Children, and the Western Temporary Home."

"All worthy causes, to be sure, but I—"

"You do realize you're all asking too much of her," came a low voice from the doorway.

Zella glanced over her shoulder to find Bert, tall and frowning, his cheeks ruddy from the cold outside. He walked into the room and folded his arms.

"She's running the most complicated publishing project Denwall's ever attempted, she's overseeing half a dozen moving parts, and she's doing it without sleep." His gaze softened as it landed on her. "You've got dark circles under your eyes."

Zella straightened. "Thank you for that."

"It wasn't an insult."

"Dark circles," she said with mock offense, "are for elderly aunts and overworked matrons. I prefer to think of them as evidence of brilliance and industry."

"That sounds like something you'd embroider on a pillow," he muttered.

Zella arched a brow, resisting a grin. "First, I don't embroider. Ever. Second, I'd be honored to help the committee with such noble causes."

"We promise you won't have to do much," Laura said. "Just attend a few meetings to add a fresh voice to the decisions and help on the day of the event. Most of the work has already been done."

Zella bobbed her head and shifted her attention to Bert. "It'll be fine. Truly. My work at Denwall won't suffer."

She might have refused the request if Bert hadn't been so dogmatic about something that didn't concern him. Now, she saw it as a challenge—and for Zella, that was far more energizing than a full night's sleep.

THIRTEEN

Bert stood near the parlor mantel with a cup of cider warming his hand. The room smelled of cinnamon and pine, and someone—likely Caro—had strung small paper stars across the arched doorways. His mother had insisted on mistletoe, and Caroline had tied ribbons around the dogs.

Bert had rolled his eyes at the silly-looking Poms. Then straightened Lily's red ribbon.

The Dennison women had left earlier that afternoon, so the noise had simmered to a low hum. Even Father had come out of his study and now paced the parlor.

When the front door finally opened again, cold air rushed in with it.

Will's deep voice rang out first, followed by the yipping of Lucy and Lily.

"They're here," Zella said, rising from the settee.

She was already halfway across the marble floor before Bert stepped one foot into the foyer.

Ivy flung her arms around Zella, who held her as if she hadn't seen her niece in years. Jemima joined in, laughing, the women's good-natured teasing already filling the space with life. Zella pulled them both close, like a mother duck gathering her flock.

Will walked farther into the entryway with his usual lopsided grin, brushing snow off his coat as he unwrapped a scarf from around his neck. He gave Zella a friendly kiss on the cheek and clapped Bert on the shoulder as he passed. "Did you leave any cookies for us, or has Ned eaten them all?"

"Caro and I agreed to save you three," Ned said as he gave Will a brotherly hug.

"Well, we're famished." Will tugged off his gloves. "And the train ride was awful. We sat across from a man who sang off-key for two entire stops."

Bert could imagine the passenger had partaken of the free beverages in the luxurious Pullman dining car. "Was it at least seasonal?"

"Oh yes," Will said with a grin. "The wrong season, however. 'Camptown Races.' Over and over."

Mother, who had been wheeled into the foyer by Father, had a wide grin on her face. It was good to see her not in pain. "Go freshen up, you three. A maid will help Ivy and Jemima get settled, then you can all come down for the tree-trimming and something to tide you over until dinner."

Soon, they began trimming the tree in the corner of the parlor. Someone dragged in a second basket of ornaments, and the floor became scattered with glass bulbs, gold cords, wooden angels, and folded paper stars.

Bert helped Jemima and Mother string popcorn.

Grandmother Shaw fell asleep in an armchair near the fireplace. When her head kept slipping, Zella took a pillow from the settee and placed it under her neck.

The gesture surprised Bert, but really, it shouldn't have. Underneath Zella's polished, extroverted exterior was a heart of gold.

Although Bert had to admit, the exterior was pretty spectacular as well.

Zella wore a gown of a deep garnet silk, the fabric catching the firelight and throwing off a warm sheen like mulled wine. Her hair, swept up in a soft chignon, had loosened just enough to let one curl slip free and graze her cheek. She tucked it back absently, and the gesture, so unguarded, made something catch in Bert's chest.

Her gray eyes, usually full of spark and mischief, had gone soft as she watched Grandmother Shaw settle more comfortably.

Truth be told, Bert couldn't look away.

Since Ivy had arrived, Zella's countenance had been radiant. She laughed often, teased Will when he hung an ornament crookedly, and showed Caroline how to cut a paper snowflake. Her sleeves were pushed up, and she'd stuck a bit of holly into her hair. When Lily jumped into her lap and nuzzled her neck, Zella gave a full-throated laugh and kissed the top of the dog's head without missing a beat. Lily's white fur was the perfect contrast to Zella's ink-black tresses.

Bert crossed his arms, half-smiling to himself. It was a little disconcerting how easily Zella fit into this house. Into his family.

Later, after supper, the guests gathered in the parlor once more. Mother settled back in her wheelchair and asked Grandmother Shaw to read from the Gospel of Luke. It had been tradition for Grandfather Shaw to have the honor on Christmas Eve, and when he passed away, his wife continued the practice.

Now wide awake after her catnap during decorating, she opened her worn Bible. The fire burned low, crackling gently. Outside the window, fat flakes drifted down in lazy spirals, blanketing the city.

Grandmother cleared her throat. Her voice, steady despite her age, filled the room with the old, familiar words.

"And she brought forth her firstborn son, and wrapped him in swaddling clothes, and laid him in a manger ..."

The room stilled. Even the dogs seemed to hold their breath.

When she read the part about the shepherds and the heavenly host, her tone softened with awe. She glanced at each of her grandchildren, as if wanting to make sure they were paying attention.

"Not in a palace, but in a stable. Not to fanfare, but to silence—until heaven could no longer contain itself. And so the angels sang. Not because the world was perfect, but because it needed hope."

Beside Bert, Zella dabbed at her eyes with the edge of her sleeve.

"God did not wait for things to be tidy or peaceful before stepping into the mess of it all," Grandmother said. "He came as light into darkness as peace into a world that had none. And He still does."

A hush followed. Caroline, at the piano, struck a quiet chord, then eased into "O Come, All Ye Faithful."

Voices rose and overlapped, all sure of the words. They moved from carol to carol, some boisterous and others reverent. "Silent Night" was the last song of the evening, and Bert's favorite.

Zella's voice emerged warm and velvet smooth. Bert barely breathed as she sang beside him, the flickering light painting shadows across her cheekbones.

They reached the third verse. The room quieted, and only Zella's voice rang out. Her eyes were closed, and Bert doubted she realized everyone had stopped to hear her sing.

"Silent night, holy night, Son of God, love's pure light. Radiant beams from Thy holy face—"

Mother sniffled. Grandmother wiped her eyes.

"—With the dawn of redeeming grace, Jesus, Lord, at Thy birth, Jesus, Lord, at Thy birth."

On the fourth and final verse, all voices in the room joined in. Father's baritone was as strong as Will's, and they complemented Zella's voice perfectly.

Just as the last note faded, Bert caught the sound of carolers outside the house. One of the household staff opened the front door. Voices, strong and steady, sang "It Came Upon the Midnight Clear."

Caroline rushed out of the parlor, her dogs on her heels. The rest of the family and guests followed. Father covered Mother with a blanket and gently pushed her wheelchair from the room and down the hall.

The wind curled into the foyer, cold and fragrant. As everyone gathered to hear the carolers, the household staff appeared, and soon the entryway was filled. They all stood, arms around each other—whether for warmth or comfort, Bert wasn't sure. Some were humming, while others sang in quiet voices.

At some point, Zella had slipped one arm through Ivy's and the other through Bert's.

Zella was so close he could smell her perfume. Sweet and airy, yet not overpowering. Lily of the Valley, maybe? Probably French.

When the carolers moved on, Zella whispered, "How lovely. It feels like all of Philadelphia has paused tonight. Just for this."

All of Philadelphia may have paused, but Bert was floored. Down for the count. And he wasn't sure he'd ever feel right-side up again.

Back inside, almost everyone scattered to their bedrooms. It was getting late. Bert lingered in the hallway outside the parlor, watching Zella and Ivy curl up on the settee by the fire, their dark heads together, whispering and smiling, looking like sisters rather than aunt and niece. Zella handed Ivy a small box, which she gently opened. Inside lay a simple brooch.

Bert told himself he should go upstairs. This was a private affair. Yet, he couldn't walk away.

"It was my mother's," Zella said quietly. "Your grandmother. I thought you should have it."

"Oh, Zella, it's beautiful."

Zella bumped Ivy's shoulder. "It's not anywhere near as nice as the jewels Will is sure to wrap you in, but Mam always loved it." She lifted her head and caught Bert watching before he could take a step back and hide in the shadows. She held his gaze for a heartbeat longer than necessary. "Bert don't go. I have something for you."

Ivy cleared her throat and rose from the settee. "I'd better head up to bed. Will's promised an early morning sleigh ride, and I don't want to oversleep." She brushed by Bert and gave him a parting wink.

Bert stepped inside and took a gaily wrapped parcel from Zella's outstretched hand.

"You didn't have to get me anything." What a fool he was for not bringing her a gift. He'd come close to buying a satin scarf in a bold floral pattern that reminded him of Zella's vibrant personality, but when he started to hand it to the salesclerk, he changed his mind and put the scarf back on the shelf.

"You've been swell these past few weeks, helping me settle in," she said.

"Even if I've drastically cut your *Styles Book* budget?"

Her lips quirked at one corner. "Oh, it wasn't that bad. I would have lost respect for you if you had just rolled over and accepted my numbers without a fight."

Bert smiled and carefully unwrapped the package to reveal a slim, leather-bound book.

The Essays of Elia, by Charles Lamb.

He ran a finger across the spine. "A first edition."

"I saw it sitting in the window of a bookshop off Pine."

"I know the one." Bert opened the cover, then searched her face. "It's a wonderful gift. Truly."

"I thought you'd appreciate a man who wrote a whole essay titled 'A Dissertation Upon Roast Pig'," she said, her tone perfectly dry.

He chuckled and nodded. "I do."

His heart thudded as he stared at her upturned face.

Thank goodness they weren't standing under mistletoe, because he would have surely bent his head and kissed her on the spot.

Fourteen

The Denwall building was quiet, its usual clatter and hum reduced to the distant groan of settling pipes. Zella pulled her coat tighter as she sat at the long worktable in the middle of the publications department, staring at a small group of illustrations that had arrived a few days earlier than she'd requested.

The radiators along the walls gave off only the faintest warmth—enough to keep the pipes from freezing, but not enough to ward off the chill that crept in under the doors. The janitor must have banked the furnace low, assuming no one would be foolish enough to work during the holiday lull.

Since the employees at Denwall's headquarters had been given New Year's Eve off, the building was like a mausoleum.

She preferred it this way.

No interruptions. Just focus.

Except she couldn't.

Her gaze drifted to the two letters sitting at the edge of the table. One she'd picked up from the Gladstone's porter on the way to Denwall. The other had been slipped under her office door in the last two days.

Florence's letter was a welcome relief. She was doing well, thank the Lord.

Zella picked up the letter and read the last paragraph one more time.

> *I'm glad you are coming for a visit, but there's no hurry. I don't think I'm that close to death. Quentin keeps hounding me to write my will, but it feels too final. Like I'm pushing my luck. I promise to write every few weeks so you won't worry about me. So proud of you, dear.*

Zella's throat tightened. Florence had always been stubbornly practical, but something in the unevenness of the handwriting made Zella uneasy. Was she as well as she claimed?

The second letter—the one she had found when she arrived two hours before—was far less welcome. Anonymous, typewritten, and nasty, the words were designed to burrow.

> You don't belong here. You'll fail miserably, and when you do, no one will hire you again.

Mean-spirited, yes, and now the second such note she'd received. But hardly actionable.

Still, it itched beneath her skin like a rash.

The clack of footsteps echoed in the hallway, drawing closer.

Bert.

Zella knew his stride now. Not too fast, and not too slow. She slid both letters under a stack of illustrations that hadn't made the final selection. The chance of him seeing them left her feeling strangely vulnerable. She didn't want his pity.

She didn't look up until he reached the threshold.

"You know," she said dryly, "if we're both spending New Year's Eve working, we might be considered more tragic than industrious."

Bert arched an eyebrow and stepped into the room. "I had to grab a file. I didn't expect to find anyone else here."

"I have illustrations to approve," she said. "The layouts are coming together faster than I expected, which means I'm probably forgetting something."

He walked to the table and carefully picked up an illustration. "These are gorgeous. That one looks like it came straight from Paris."

"You have a good eye. And yes, it did."

He took the seat across from her. "Have you heard anything from the freelance writer there?"

"She's promised to send copy in the next week. A scandalous piece on bicycling outfits with bloomers and uncovered ankles."

He chuckled and leaned back. "I understand you and Caroline have everything organized for the theatre party on the third?"

"Your mother finalized the guest list, and I accompanied Caroline to the milliner to find the right hat to go with her pretty new gown. Caroline is worried no one will attend, but I think she'll be pleasantly surprised. I can't imagine anyone resisting a private box at the Chestnut Street Opera House." She hesitated, not entirely sure why she needed to know, but she asked anyway. "Are you coming to the theatre party?"

"I wouldn't miss it." He stretched his long legs and placed his hands behind his head. "And what about tonight? It's New Year's Eve. Are you doing anything?" he asked casually.

Zella shook her head. "No. With Ivy, Will, and Jemima back in New York, I'll be spending the evening alone."

Bert frowned.

"Don't feel sorry for me. I detest all the sentimental toasts and silly resolutions."

"No resolutions?" He grinned. "I'm surprised."

"I don't believe in making promises I don't intend to keep." She gave him a sidelong look. "You?"

"I make them," he said. "But only the kind I know I'll never break."

She snickered. "That's very bold of you."

His eyes lingered on her for a moment, and he tilted his head. "If you were in New York right now, would there be a special someone you'd spend New Year's Eve with?"

What was he asking, exactly?

"What do you mean?"

"A ... fellow. Back in New York. Do you have one?"

She deliberately gave him a slow, secretive smile. "Why do you want to know?"

He shrugged, but the tips of his ears pinkened. "Just wondering how many hearts you've broken by being in Philadelphia this season."

Someone had once told her it was wise to leave a man wondering. And although she typically enjoyed teasing the stoic Bert, it didn't sit right just now.

"None worth counting," she answered as she went back to her work. "These are some illustrations for the home décor layout. The dining room of a British peer of the realm." Zella reached for a second portfolio and pushed it toward him.

Bert opened the folio and inspected the sketch, then shifted his hazel eyes on her. "I've got to hand it to you. You know what you're doing. I was skeptical about this section, but I think customers will love it."

Zella's heart constricted at the praise. Why did such a simple comment turn her insides to jelly?

She strove for a lighthearted tone. "Imagine all the women flooding into Denwall with the magazine open to this illustration, trying to buy goods that will make their homes look like that of an English aristocrat."

"Like I said, you're good at what you do."

She gazed at the quiet steadiness in his expression. "Thank you."

He shrugged. "It's just the truth."

"Since we're being honest and complimentary, I think you're excellent at what you do as well." When he just smiled, she pressed on. "Do you imagine yourself in the head office?"

Bert leaned forward, resting his forearms on the table. "I didn't want the job before Father retired, nor do I want it now. I've never wanted the top spot."

"Do you think Ballard will become permanent?" She studied him carefully.

"No, I think he wants to move back home. Be closer to his family. But I think Max will run Denwall someday, and when he does, he'll be smart and visionary enough to keep people like you close."

"Even though I'm a woman?"

"Denwall couldn't ask for a better person to run this project."

"Thank you." Her voice came out breathily.

He gave a cheeky grin. "Besides, you're a lot prettier than any man they could put in this position."

FIFTEEN

Bert walked through the marble vestibule and paused just inside the rotunda of the Chestnut Street Opera House. Rich velvet hangings in maroon and gold softened the towering walls, their ornate folds catching the glow of what must be a hundred lights on a domed chandelier.

The air hummed with conversation, silk skirts rustling across the marble floors as society's finest drifted between the ladies' retiring room and the gentlemen's smoking parlor.

His parents and the Dennisons had procured one of the four proscenium boxes for the theatre party held in honor of Caro and Alix. Because of Mother's injury—although she was getting better by the day—she had relegated the final planning to Zella. Father, who didn't want to attend the party without Mother, asked Bert to go in his stead.

The proscenium box was situated more like a private salon than part of a public theatre, with plush maroon velvet armchairs arranged in rows on an Oriental carpet.

The debutantes had claimed the front row, naturally. Their gloved hands grasped the curved balcony rail as they peered at the stage below. Behind them lounged the five young bachelors, including Ned, who had already earned a warning glance from Lena for making some wry remark about the private lives of actresses.

Bert sat farther back, behind and to the left of Zella and Lena. To his right, James and Myra conversed in low tones, the theatre lights catching on Myra's diamonds when she moved.

Despite the box's grandeur of maroon velvet and canary satin, with frescoes of birds and vines adorning the walls, Bert couldn't help watching Zella instead. Despite her navy blue silk and modest pearls, she outshone every woman in the place. Of course, that was just his opinion.

His gaze caught on her profile. She didn't glance his way, but something about the angle of her chin made him wonder if she knew he was watching.

"Quite the crowd tonight," he heard Zella say to Lena, as she raised her opera glasses. "I wonder how many people are here for the performance and how many think *they* are the show."

Lena giggled the most lighthearted laugh he'd heard from her in a long while.

The lights dimmed as the orchestra swelled, the strings pulling the audience into the story before a single word was spoken. Velvet curtains parted to reveal the first scene of the play *Madame Sans-Gêne*, set in a laundry shop in Paris in 1792. Bert knew some of the story of Catherine Hübscher, an outspoken French laundress who became the Duchess of Danzig and a friend of Napoleon himself.

The lead actress stepped onto the stage with commanding grace, her voice ringing clear across the opera house. Her movements were bold, even exaggerated, but there was charm in it, and she delivered her clever dialogue with flair.

During intermission, the young men conversed with the young ladies in the vestibule. When they returned to their seats, George Whitby leaned over the balcony, pointing out something in the audience below to Alix.

Ned nudged Whitby with his elbow. "Careful, sir. If you lean any farther, you'll tumble straight into the first violinist."

Again, Bert noticed Ned's attention on Alix. The two had always been the best of friends, despite the two-year age difference. Yet something more was going on here.

Before Bert could think on it further, the third act opened in a flurry of stage movement. Set in Napoleon's court, the costumes were more elaborate, and the comedic timing of the actors kept the audience engaged.

Although he'd stood during intermission, Bert's legs needed stretching again. When he shifted, Zella gave him a mock scowl. He almost burst out laughing. She could rival any formidable schoolmarm.

During one scene, Catherine was ridiculed for her lowly beginnings, but she stood her ground. The actress continued in a rustic accent, pointing out that many others, including Napoleon's sisters, had humble beginnings.

"We are all laundresses here," she said with defiant clarity. "Only I don't pretend otherwise."

Bert winced. There were a number of people in the audience who'd risen far in Philadelphia society yet had the arrogance to look down their noses at others. Truth be told, he could sometimes see that trait in his father.

The final curtain fell to generous applause. The cast took their bows, and Bert couldn't help but scan for Zella's reaction. She applauded, but her smile seemed stiff.

Had she not enjoyed the performance?

Outside, the gas lamps lit the snow in soft halos, flakes clinging to overcoats and elaborate millinery. The crowd funneled into the night in murmuring waves. The younger of their party guests piled into the first two carriages, their voices still bubbling with commentary and laughter.

Bert joined James and Myra near the last carriage. James started to shoo the young men into a vehicle separate from the debutantes, but Myra placed a gloved hand on his arm.

"Leave it, James. It's only a five-minute ride to the restaurant. They'll be fine. Ned is in the first, and he'll look out for Alexandra and Caroline. And Helena's in the second."

Bert couldn't fault Myra's logic. Ned would indeed be a more than suitable watchdog. And no young man would dare try something inappropriate while Lena was watching them.

Zella joined Bert at the edge of the sidewalk while James helped Myra into the carriage. Zella pulled her fur cape snug around her neck and smiled faintly when she turned toward him.

"Enjoy the performance?" Bert asked, offering his hand to help her in.

"More than I thought I would," she said. "Though I suspect you found parts unbearable."

"Only the overacting in the soirée scene."

She gave a soft laugh as she ducked her head to climb into the carriage. "You mean the socializing of the upper crust?"

"Especially the socializing." Bert took the seat beside her, across the aisle from James and Myra, his knees accidentally touching Zella's as the carriage lurched forward.

"Well," Myra sighed, snuggling into her husband's side, "our guests all seemed to enjoy themselves."

"No one eloped. That counts as a success," James added dryly.

Zella tilted her head toward Bert, a grin tugging at her lips. "So, did the play not meet your lofty standards, Mr. Walraven?"

Bert gave a low laugh. "Let's say it took liberties with the truth."

"I rather liked the liberties," Zella said. "Sometimes the truth is easier to accept when it's gilded a little."

Why didn't that attitude surprise him? Had Zella ever gilded the truth herself—just enough to make it more palatable?

———

Zella smoothed a hand over her skirt as she took her seat beside Myra at the long table reserved for their party. The Bellevue Hotel's dining room glowed with warm elegance, all polished mahogany and creamy marble, the air humming with the quiet murmur of conversation and the occasional clink of crystal.

Caroline and Alix sat at the far end with the other debutantes, chatting excitedly and caught up in the glitter of it all. Their voices rang with unguarded excitement, their glances often flicking toward the young men seated nearby. They were radiant with optimism Zella admired but couldn't quite summon.

"Alexandra seems quite taken with George Whitby's attention," Myra murmured, following Zella's gaze.

"She's not watching George, however," Zella said quietly.

"What do you mean?"

"She's watching Ned. Even when she laughs with George."

"Well. That could get interesting."

"I suspect it will, eventually."

Myra tilted her head. "Were you like them at that age?"

Zella hesitated, her smile tightening. "No. I was never that young."

The comment slipped out before she could weigh it, but beside her, Bert cleared his throat. "What did you mean by that?" Something unreadable flickered behind his spectacles.

Zella stirred her soup. "Nothing. Just that I didn't debut."

"That's not what you said."

She looked at him then, full on. "Some girls are allowed to

be soft and wide-eyed. Others learn early that survival means keeping your chin up and your heart behind lock and key."

Bert didn't flinch. He simply inclined his head, the kind of acknowledgment that didn't demand more than she wanted to give.

"I'm sorry," she said quietly. "That was rather dramatic. I blame the wine. It can make one philosophical."

"Then I should avoid it."

Her lips twitched in spite of herself.

The waiter returned with the next course of roast pheasant, duchess potatoes piped in rosettes, and tender asparagus with hollandaise. The room buzzed again as forks clinked and light conversation resumed. The young people discussed the merits of the play they'd seen.

"The third act was the best," George Whitby declared from farther down the table. "Though I still don't understand why the laundress couldn't just pretend to fit in. It wouldn't have killed her to act the part of a duchess, rather than stand out like a sore thumb in a ballroom of Napoleon's court."

"That's the whole point," Alix said, surprising Zella with her clarity. "She wasn't ashamed of where she came from, and she wouldn't start pretending just because they gave her a title."

Zella ran a finger along the top of her wineglass. "We are all laundresses here. Only some of us *do* choose to forget it."

A few chuckled. Others blinked, probably unsure whether to be amused or insulted. Myra tilted her head, but Zella offered no further explanation. She'd meant it as self-deprecation—a reversal of the play's line—but now wondered if others had taken it as a slight. If only she'd kept quiet a moment longer.

Unease twisted in her chest.

Pretending. That was exactly what she did. Every day. A

widow's life had proved excellent camouflage. It gave her freedom, distance, dignity. But at what cost?

Although she didn't turn her head, she felt Bert's gaze as it rested on her. Adept at reading others' thoughts, he probably sensed she was a fraud.

Between courses, the waiters swept in with practiced grace to clear dishes and offer coffee. Zella declined the dessert—a molded custard with spun sugar—and instead accepted a demitasse of coffee with cream.

Bert dug into the custard with enthusiasm, and she grinned at how he loved his sweets.

The quiet between them now was more comfortable, companionable even.

"You know," he said in a low voice meant only for her, "you're not as guarded as you think."

Zella raised a brow. "I beg your pardon?"

"You said earlier that you keep your heart behind lock and key. I don't think that's entirely true."

"Don't go soft on me, Walraven."

"Too late," he said. "I already admire your debating skills. Now I suspect there's an actual heart under all that starch and wit."

Zella chuckled, but the warmth in her chest surprised her. "Well, keep that to yourself. I have a reputation to uphold."

She lifted her coffee cup again, but her eyes drifted down to where Bert's hand rested casually on the white linen cloth. His knuckles were red and scuffed, the skin near one joint raw, like he'd scraped it recently. She blinked, then looked again. Several of his knuckles bore signs of abuse, old and new. Tiny bruises. Faint lines where the skin had split and healed.

"You've been fighting," she said, not quite a question.

He followed her gaze, then pulled his hand back as if she'd caught him pilfering.

"I've taken up boxing," he said at last, in that same low voice.

Zella leaned slightly closer. "Let me guess. At a gentlemen's club with leather gloves and rules no one really follows?"

He gave a half-smile. "Something like that."

She watched him for a long moment, reading beneath the deflection. "Farm boys used to do the same thing where I grew up," she said. "They'd pummel each other behind the hay barn, thinking it made them tough. Or thinking they'd be the next John Sullivan, champion of the world."

His eyes narrowed slightly, but not in anger. It was more like a slight warning to cease and desist.

She pressed on, quiet and steady. "But this isn't about sport, is it? This is about what happened to you in Madison Square Park."

He looked away, jaw tight. A breath passed, then he searched her face once more. "I never want to feel that helpless again."

Something shifted in her heart. "You weren't helpless, Bert. You were caught off guard. That's not the same thing as being weak."

He let out a sharp breath, more of a scoff. "It felt the same."

Zella nodded slowly. "Of course it did. That's the lie fear tells us—that being vulnerable once means we always will be."

She reached out, hesitated, then touched his hand lightly, her fingers brushing the edge of his battered knuckles.

"You're already strong. Probably always have been. You don't need your fists to prove it."

His gaze met hers again, and something shifted in it— something less guarded. "And what would you have me use instead?"

She tilted her head. "The Bert I know has a better weapon

than his fists. He uses his mind. His loyalty. His wit, though he hides it behind accounting ledgers and spectacles."

"You think I'm witty?"

"I think you're dangerous when you choose to be. In the best possible way."

He didn't speak, but the edge of his mouth curved.

Then his hand turned over, just enough to curl his fingers lightly around hers. Not a grasp, not a claim. Just an acknowledgment.

Across the table, someone called Zella's name, and she withdrew her hand, carefully smoothing her napkin over her lap.

But the connection lingered.

Sixteen

Once Bert had accidentally let it slip that he was boxing at the Liberty Athletic Club, Max joined too, and began showing up at regular intervals. He was quite good, actually, which shouldn't have surprised Bert. Apparently, he'd taken up the sport several years earlier.

Like Bert, Max claimed he appreciated the atmosphere, so different from the men's clubs their fathers frequented. At Liberty, no cigar smoke choked the foyer. No constant chatter about investments or misspent inheritances filled the gymnasium.

Here, the air was heavy with effort, not ego. The scent of liniment and sawdust clung to the walls, mingling with the odor of exertion. No one cared about your name here. Just your footwork.

Bert rolled his shoulders, the ache in his left arm still singing from that last round. Max, entirely too cheerful for a man who'd just been hit in the ribs, was dressing beside him in the locker room. The gym's buzz faded behind the heavy oak door.

"You've improved," Max said, nodding toward the gymnasium. "You're not leading with your chin anymore."

"Encouraging," Bert muttered, wincing as he pulled on a fresh shirt. He buttoned his collar and gave Max a pointed look—one meant to make him squirm. "So, are you still courting the lovely Miss Donovan?"

Max's eyes grew wide. "Who said I was courting her?"

"Your stepmother."

Max sighed and slipped his jacket on. "Well, Myra is wrong. Miss Donovan and I attended the season opening of the museum together, but that was all."

"No interest in anything more?"

"Miss Donovan, although one of the loveliest young women in Philadelphia, has about as much intelligence as a turnip."

Bert let out a low whistle. "No holds barred there, my friend."

"I said she was lovely." Max grinned his signature smile that had broken many females' hearts. "But I don't enjoy conversations that feel like I'm teaching a lamb to read."

Bert chuckled and slapped Max on the back. "One of these days, someone is going to knock you off your feet."

"You're headed for the same fate," Max said as they stepped out of the athletic club and onto the sidewalk.

It was still early morning, so when Bert raised his hand to hail a hansom cab, one was soon nosing its way toward them.

Max folded his tall frame into the carriage seat across from Bert. "You doing anything Thursday evening?"

"Probably sitting at home with a good book. Why?"

"There's a private exhibit preview at the Steuben Gallery. You might be interested. It's a limited guest list, but I'm sure I could convince the curator to let you in," Max said with a wink.

"Since when do you enjoy standing around with wine-drunk patrons pretending to understand brushstrokes?"

"The hall outside my office needs some artwork. Someone recommended this showing." He casually swiped at his pristine jacket sleeve. "I invited Mrs. Capp to join me."

Bert stared at Max, who had yet to look up from the most interesting piece of lint ever seen by man. When did Max and Zella start doing things together? Outside of work, that is. "You're going with Zella?"

"Mm." Max's voice was maddeningly casual. "Thought it might be good inspiration. You know—French interiors, decorative motifs. She's got an eye for those things."

Bert tried not to let it show, but something cold and sharp settled in his gut. "You two spending a lot of time together?"

"Now and then." Max glanced at Bert and shrugged. "She's clever. Beautiful. But of course, you know that."

What game was Max playing?

"She keeps her own counsel, though." Max frowned. "You never really know what she's thinking."

"Maybe *you* don't." The words came out before Bert could rein them in.

Max tilted his head, amused. "*You* do?"

"I was referring to Ivy. She knows Zella better than anyone." *Nice deflection, Bert, you fool.* "Myself, I don't make a habit of speculating what's going on in any woman's head, let alone Mrs. Capp's."

"No," Max said with a grin. "But you watch her like she's a puzzle you're trying to solve."

Bert said nothing. He wasn't about to give Max the satisfaction.

Because he *did* study her. Zella was brilliant and unpredictable and maddening. And the idea of Max escorting her to a private exhibit, discussing brushwork and lighting, stirred something deep and unreasonable within him.

He didn't want Zella to fall for Max's charms when the man had no intention of marrying. Max strove for a carefree existence above all else.

But concern for her heart wasn't all that flashed through Bert. He could admit that much. To himself, anyway.

It was none of his business, a part of him whispered. Zella wasn't his. She wasn't anyone's.

Still, he couldn't help the thought creeping in that she hadn't mentioned the exhibit when he saw her yesterday. Or the day before that. Why not?

"Let me know if you want an invitation," Max said as the carriage stopped outside the Denwall office building.

"I'm sure you'll represent Denwall just fine."

Max gave him a wink. And with that, he hopped from the carriage, leaving Bert staring at Max's back and wondering how his life had gone so far off the rails.

He didn't like private art exhibits.

But he liked the idea of Zella and Max attending one together—possibly arm in arm—even less.

The Steuben Gallery wasn't the grandest space in Philadelphia, but it had charm. Its gaslight sconces bathed the gilded frames in a warm, honeyed glow, and the soft echo of footfalls on polished oak floors gave the whole place an air of reverence.

Zella stood, gloved hands clasped behind her back, in front of a study of a woman in repose on a settee in a French drawing room. The furniture in the piece appeared far too delicate for actual use. Still, the painting was perfectly composed, and Zella's mind immediately flicked to how it might work in the centerfold of the *Styles Book*.

Across the gallery, Max was deep in conversation with a young artist about pigment choices, while Lena, dressed in an elegant periwinkle walking gown, stood at Zella's side, murmuring her own observations. "The painting is too reminiscent of the one by Alfred Stevens. The Belgian painter, not the British painter of the same name."

Zella turned and stared at Lena. Her new friend was like an onion, with layers that, when peeled back, revealed more layers. "True," she said with a nod. "But there's something more here. Something different from Stevens's work. Look at the balance of the lighting. That sconce there. See how it pulls your eye into the room?"

Lena leaned in. "Ah. That's why Max brought you. He needs someone with vision, not just someone who buys paintings because they match the rug."

Zella smiled faintly, but her eyes remained on the artwork. "It's peaceful here. I needed that."

"I figured you did." Lena glanced at her sideways. "Have you been sleeping?"

No, not really. Things weren't going as smoothly as Zella would like. It wasn't any one thing that caused her to wonder if they'd launch the magazine on time, but dozens of little things. Delays. Mishaps. She still felt like she was waiting for the other shoe to drop, her nerves stretched taut beneath the surface.

"I'll be all right."

Lena didn't press. She only looped her arm gently through Zella's and tipped her head toward the next room. "Come on. There's a series of dogs in dresses on display. You'll love them."

They were halfway into the second salon when Zella paused. Her gaze snagged on a familiar figure near the entrance —broad-shouldered, mussed chestnut hair, wire-framed spectacles perched on his nose.

Her breath caught.

What was Bert doing at the showing?

He'd never mentioned he was attending. And why should he? She wasn't his friend or confidante but just a subordinate at his family's business.

Had he brought someone with him? A woman, perhaps? The wayward thought caused Zella's stomach to clench.

He was scanning the room, hands in his pockets, his expression unreadable as ever. But when his eyes landed on her, he didn't look away.

Neither did Zella.

"I'll give you two a moment," Lena said lightly, slipping away before Zella could protest.

Bert approached at a measured pace, and when he stopped beside her, he scanned the room.

"You never mentioned you were coming to this," he said quietly.

Zella arched a brow. "Neither did you."

"I heard about it from Max."

"Ah," she said. "So you were curious."

"Something like that."

They stood in silence for a moment, looking at a watercolor of a flower shop. The storefront was shaded in lilac tones, the awning half-blown in the wind. It was delicate, dreamy.

Zella spotted Max and Lena on the other side of the room, their red heads close together in suspect conversation. Lena smacked Max on the arm with her fan, and he laughed.

Bert cleared his throat. "Why do I have the feeling I've been hoodwinked?"

"What do you mean?"

"It's nothing." But he glared at Max, who shot him a wink.

Whatever was going on, it was between Bert and Max. Zella suspected Lena was an innocent party in the whole affair.

Bert tipped his chin and stared down at her, as if trying to figure out a train schedule.

His lovely eyes and chiseled jaw had her feeling slightly derailed.

"So, how's the Charity Ball Committee faring?"

She sucked in a breath. "Fine."

"Really?"

Zella sighed and shrugged. She wasn't surprised by the cold shoulder of some of the committee members, yet it hurt anyway. "No, it's not fine. But it will be, come event night. You get a group of society matrons working together, and there are bound to be fireworks. Too many generals and not enough corporals."

"I've heard my mother say something similar many times."

Zella tilted her head. "Are you going to grace us with your presence at the ball?"

"I'll be there. Mother, and probably you and Caroline, will have my head on a platter if I don't show."

"I wouldn't hold it against you, but I agree Caroline might. She needs all the reinforcements she can get."

"Are you worried about her?" His voice took on an edge she didn't hear very often. "Should I be concerned that someone might bother her? A young man, perhaps?"

Zella placed a hand on his arm. How fortunate Caroline was to have such a caring brother. "It's nothing like that. My goodness, you're like an overprotective papa bear."

"When it comes to my sister, yes, I am."

"Well, not to worry. I just meant that Caroline will feel more at ease knowing her family is nearby. I've written and asked Will and Ivy to attend as well. And Ned will come if I have to drag him there."

"Speaking of overprotective."

She felt his warm smile all the way to her toes.

Lena and Max finally wandered over to join them.

"I think I've seen enough," Max declared. "It's getting late. Ready to go, Mrs. Capp? Bert?"

"I'll walk Mrs. Capp home, if you like," Bert said.

Zella swallowed. Why did the idea of walking along a quiet, lamplit street with Bert cause her heart to thud? "That's very chivalrous of you, but my apartment is just around the corner."

"I insist."

They said their goodbyes to the Dennisons on the sidewalk outside the gallery. Max hailed a hansom cab, and he and his sister climbed in.

Bert pulled Zella's hand through his arm, though he didn't move in too close.

Shame, that.

They walked in silence until they reached the Gladstone's front door.

Lamplight shone on his hair as his eyes lingered on her. "I'm headed to our Chicago store for a few days, so I guess the next time I see you will be at the ball."

Zella hadn't realized he was going out of town. Why did she have the feeling that she'd miss him?

The doorman, who waited like a good soldier for the apartment tenants to come and go, tipped his hat. "Good evening, Mrs. Capp."

"Good evening." She pulled her arm from Bert's, but not before giving his hand a pat. "Have a safe trip. See you Saturday."

His eyes were warm and unflinching. "Save me a dance."

Seventeen

The Academy of Music, with its gilded balconies and rose-colored velvet seats, echoed with the sounds of people at work, striving to make the Charity Ball the best it could be.

The grand chandelier, its thousand crystals catching the late afternoon light, had been freshly polished for the occasion, and the marble foyer smelled faintly of beeswax.

In the auditorium, where the largest society event of the year would take place, a frenzy of florists, caterers, and society volunteers wove around each other like threads in a tapestry. Some were pulled taut, while others frayed at the edges.

Zella moved through it all, trying to be helpful without taking over or being pushy, which was her usual *modus operandi*. The ball was in less than ten hours, but despite the lateness, the auditorium still rang with the clatter of ladders and the rustle of silk ribbon being draped over banisters. The movable theatre seats had been hidden beneath floorboards by the competent academy staff.

Mrs. Holcroft, one of the more unlikeable of the society matrons, snapped her fingers in Zella's direction as if summoning a footman.

"Mrs. Capp, would you be a dearie and check with the florist again? The garland by the musicians' platform is crooked, and I was assured symmetry."

Zella smiled. Polite. Pleasant. Unbothered.

Or at least she tried to appear that way.

Inside, she'd begun to tally how many times she'd been called *dearie*, *my girl*, or *capable*. The count was at fourteen.

She turned from the half-finished stage and wove her way past a trio of debutantes practicing their curtsies in the far corner. Alix Dennison shot her a bright, conspiratorial grin.

"You'd think the committee expects you to levitate the orchestra next," she whispered.

Zella laughed softly, the tension in her belly loosening just enough to breathe again. "Don't give them ideas. If I'm still standing by the first dance, it'll be a miracle."

"You'll look glorious. I peeked at your gown," Alix said. "Gold satin? Bold choice. You'll outshine half the room."

"Well, let's hope I don't blind the strings section."

Behind them, a harried staff member rushed past carrying a tray of freshly polished silverware. Someone nearby remarked that the silver was smudged and unsuitable for the night's dinner guests. Another woman clucked her tongue and replied, "Well, I'm sure the capable Mrs. Capp can help with that."

Count fifteen.

Zella didn't flinch. But the backhanded comment, one of many, landed.

To be sure, none of them were outright insults. Not exactly. It was the sarcastic gratitude, the casual condescension, the way they thanked her like they might a well-trained butler. Never quite including her. Never quite letting her forget she wasn't one of them.

"Oh, Mrs. *Caauhpp*?" a voice sing-songed as she passed. Mrs. Winthrop, tall and bony, possessed a penchant for unnecessarily stretching out the vowels in people's names. "The violinist has requested a footstool. Do see to it."

Zella inclined her head. "Of course."

As she moved to leave, Alix leaned in again. "If anyone orders you around one more time, I'll stage a fainting spell and knock over several floral arrangements to cause a commotion. Just say the word."

"Tempting," Zella murmured.

She crossed the ballroom toward a floral display, heels clicking on the parquet floor. Her gown for tonight was already hanging in a quiet upstairs dressing room, and for a moment she let herself imagine how she might feel walking into the finished auditorium not as a subordinate workhorse, but as a guest. Not as a useful woman, but a woman *seen*.

"Zella?" came a gentle voice behind her.

Myra approached, her expression soft. She wore a lilac silk morning jacket with fur trim and a matching hat perched just so.

"I wanted to thank you, my dear," Myra said, and there was no flattery in her tone, just warmth. "This ball would be chaos without your help. And I know not everyone's said as much."

Zella hesitated. "Thank you, Myra. That means more than you know."

"James says he's never seen the Charity Ball so organized. He suspects you may have frightened the committee into competence."

"Only mildly intimidated," Zella replied, lips quirking.

Myra chuckled and touched her arm. "Don't let them wear you down. You belong here." Before Zella could formulate a reply, Myra swept off, leaving only the faint scent of rose perfume behind.

Her attention back on the garlands, Zella inspected the slanted arrangement. It was, in fact, crooked.

She gestured to one of the florist's assistants. "Ladder, please." Rather than asking the overworked young man to complete the task, she did it herself. If you wanted something done right ...

She climbed to the top rung and shifted the right side of the garland an inch higher. "How's that?"

The young man nodded. "Looks good, Mrs. Capp."

She returned to terra firma, placing a hand on her lower back.

Mrs. Capp. Coming from the mouth of this young person made her sound old. Almost as old as her back felt.

What would he say, she wondered, if she told him she wasn't a widow at all? Would he be surprised?

What would *any* of them say? Would they whisper? Snub her outright?

Lately, the question often popped into her mind the more she brushed shoulders with Philadelphia society.

And what of Denwall? Would the magazine lose credibility if the managing director whom they'd lauded in local newspaper interviews turned out to have lied about her identity?

She hadn't intended to lie for more than a few months when she first thought of the idea all those years before, just until she got her career started. But when the truth became too complicated to explain, the lie settled in like dust in old drapes.

Now, the stakes were higher.

By keeping quiet, she wasn't just protecting herself anymore. She was protecting the Dennison and Walraven families. Protecting *Bert.*

The thought of him stirred something fragile inside her.

If I say something now, will it all unravel?

She didn't need society's approval. She didn't even want it, or so she told herself.

Still, it would be nice to be accepted for who she really

was. A woman who'd run from an abusive father to build something of her own. A successful life, carved from nothing but desperation and determination.

Will Ivy forgive me when I tell her the truth? She'd be hurt, certainly. But she'd forgive. That was her nature.

But these women? The ones who called her *capable* and *my girl*? They'd most likely never let her forget the deception.

Zella looked once more at the garland, now straightened and symmetrical. Satisfactory.

This evening, she would make her entrance in a gold satin gown that had cost her a month's wages, her head held high. But the sting from the day's slights would still hum beneath the surface.

And the truth? The truth was waiting for her to take the first tentative step.

She fervently prayed she wouldn't tumble so hard that she'd never get back up.

***

Music filled the auditorium, and everywhere Bert looked, Philadelphia's elite flitted from one group to the next. In the Academy of Music's cheap seats, which the committee sold at a dollar each, people could come and watch the ball below. But they couldn't take part themselves. Amazingly, every ticket had sold.

He searched the makeshift ballroom for his family, but spotted Zella instead.

She was standing near the foot of the grand staircase, enduring what seemed to be a one-sided conversation with two women he recognized from the charity committee.

Zella wore a shimmering gold satin gown the color of champagne with an effortless grace she always seemed to possess, her black hair swept up with jeweled pins that caught the light.

But Bert could see the distress in her eyes—the tight smile, the way her gloved fingers flexed ever so slightly around her dance card, the faint tilt of her chin. Not defiant, but close.

He stepped nearer, just in time to hear Mrs. Holcroft's crisp tone. "Of course, we're grateful for your assistance with the festivities. It was helpful to have someone familiar with how to manage the help."

Zella inclined her head. "You're very welcome."

"And that entrance arch you suggested turned out so charming. We were all quite relieved it didn't fall."

The women tittered.

Bert clenched his jaw. He knew that syrupy tone of dismissive politeness society women used when they wanted to remind someone of their place.

Mrs. Langley added, "And it's nice to see you've stayed for the ball. We thought you'd have left to return to your apartment by now."

Zella's countenance didn't waver. "Mrs. Dennison insisted I stay."

"Well," Mrs. Holcroft said, brushing a gloved hand down her sleeve, "do enjoy the evening. I'm sure there are many here tonight you'll recognize. Of course, you'll have to wait until after the first waltz to step onto the floor."

The barb hung in the air. The first dance of the evening was for committee members, their spouses, and city dignitaries. Despite her efforts as a temporary committee member, the women still didn't believe that Zella belonged.

The nasty women drifted off in a cloud of condescension.

The strains of the first waltz began.

Zella shifted slightly, her posture still perfect, but her eyes blazed.

Bert saw it then. The hurt quickly buried beneath anger,

and then smoothed over again into composure. A whole storm, hidden behind a perfectly still mask.

He didn't think. He just crossed the ballroom in five long strides and stopped directly in front of her.

"Dance with me," he said.

Zella stared. "Excuse me?"

He extended his hand, palm up. "Dance with me. Right now. Don't argue."

"Is this a rescue?"

"Yes," he said plainly.

She arched a brow and placed her hand in his. "Well. When you put it that way."

He led her onto the floor as the orchestra played the stately waltz, and all around them, heads turned. He and Zella weren't exactly the couple of the hour, but people noticed. The Walraven name held weight. Bert didn't use it often, but when he did, he used it precisely.

And tonight, he used it for her.

Zella danced like she was born to it—with poise, control, and precision. Yet, he felt the way her fingers curled just slightly against his shoulder. The way her breath caught when he guided her into a turn.

"You didn't have to dance with me," she said quietly.

"I know."

"But I appreciate it."

He gave a tight smile. "I thought it might irritate the Langleys."

"It did, if the pinched look on Mrs. Langley's face is any indication."

"Excellent."

They moved in silence for a few more bars, and then she said, "You know this only fuels gossip."

"Let them talk."

"You're not afraid of them?" She peered up at him with

those lovely eyes.

He met her gaze steadily. "No. Although I'm a little afraid of you."

She looked away, thrown off for just a moment.

And Bert felt it—that strange, electric pull between them. Not flashy. Not dramatic. Just solid and real, like something forged slowly, carefully, in fire.

When the dance ended, he bowed low and kissed her gloved hand.

Her mouth formed an *O*, like he'd surprised her again.

He prayed it was in a good way.

Bert tucked Zella's arm through his, and they strolled from the dance floor.

Zella peered up at him and said in a low voice, "Do you mind performing one more rescue this evening? There's a little service balcony off the dressing hall. It's not meant for guests, but I need air."

"Of course." He pulled her gently toward the stairs.

Why did he feel like he was on the precipice of a moment that would change his life forever?

———

They made their way to the third floor and slipped behind a velvet curtain near the staircase. Zella pushed on a door, and it creaked open. They stepped onto a narrow iron platform high above Locust Street.

She hadn't expected the small balcony to feel so intimate. Cold air prickled her skin.

Bert unbuttoned his jacket, slipped his arms from its sleeves, and placed it around Zella's shoulders.

The gentlemanly gesture made her heart skip a beat. She

pulled the jacket tight around her. "Thank you. Three rescues in one day. I'm not used to it."

"You didn't really need my help."

"Then why did you do it?"

"Because I was angry." Light from a streetlamp glinted off his spectacles, making it difficult to read his expression.

She placed a hand on her chest. "Angry at me?"

"No," Bert said quickly. "At them."

He stepped closer. "I've watched you carry the Denwall project, Caroline's debut, and this event, with more grace than half of Philadelphia society combined. Yet they treat you like you're less."

Zella crossed her arms around her middle. "I don't think they even realize they're treating me that way."

"That doesn't make it right."

"And was our dance supposed to fix it?"

"I don't know," he admitted. "But I wanted people to see what I see when I look at you."

Her breath caught in her throat, and she swallowed. "And how is that, Mr. Walraven? How do you see me?"

His jaw worked for a moment. "I see you as someone who belongs anywhere she wants to stand."

For a long moment, neither of them moved.

What's going on here?

She hadn't planned this conversation. This moment. Yet it felt right. "You make things difficult, you know."

"I have that effect."

She ignored his quip. "I came here to further my career. Not to get entangled."

"Too late," he said.

He didn't move in any closer but gazed out over the street.

She watched him. His quiet intensity filling empty spaces in her heart.

And for the first time in a very long time, she didn't feel like she had to defend herself or smooth the edges. To pretend.

He shifted slightly, his forearm brushing hers.

The touch wasn't improper. Not really. But she felt it everywhere.

"I used to think I'd never run out of words," she said quietly. "That if I kept talking, people wouldn't question whether I belonged in the room."

He stared at her behind his wire-rimmed spectacles, never blinking like he was afraid he'd miss something.

"But lately, I've realized that the only people who really matter don't need to be convinced."

The softest smile touched his mouth.

"I might have needed a nudge at first," he said. "But then I just sat back in awe and watched you work. And it knocked the wind out of me."

The compliment sent a ripple through her chest so sudden and warm, she couldn't breathe.

"Bert—"

But whatever she'd meant to say vanished when he stepped just a little closer. He removed his spectacles and stuck them in the pocket of the jacket that hung around her shoulders.

He didn't rush. He didn't ask. He just looked at her with a quiet, steady gaze. When she didn't move, didn't stop him, he lifted one hand and brushed her cheek with the backs of his fingers.

Her breath caught.

And then he leaned in and kissed her. It wasn't dramatic or rushed. It was honest. Certain. The kind of kiss that didn't ask for permission so much as offer a promise.

I see you. I want you. No performance. No pretending.

Zella let her eyes close, her hands tightening slightly on the lapels of the jacket that hung around her shoulders.

Everything around them faded. The only sounds were the

soft rustle of his coat and the hum of music from the auditorium.

When he finally pulled back, it was only by an inch. Their foreheads nearly touched.

"I shouldn't have done that," he said, though his voice didn't sound regretful.

"I'm glad you did," she whispered.

He smiled, a little uneven, a little stunned. "Well. That's something."

Zella stepped back first, breathless in the best way.

"We should go," she said, but made no move to leave.

"In a minute." He reached gently for her hand and kissed her once again.

Eighteen

The Denwall building was still and quiet, the kind of quiet Zella had come to enjoy in the last few weeks. Staff came in and out of her office constantly, and decisions needed to be made on the spot. There was usually so much noise that it was sometimes difficult to think.

She loved every minute, but sometimes she just needed people to leave her alone.

Except for the one person she rarely saw.

Bert had left at the beginning of February to tour shipping facilities with the logistics director, and Zella didn't see him for almost three weeks. At least he'd sent her a postcard from Milwaukee. Something witty and not the least bit sentimental.

Once he returned, not much changed. Both were so busy there was barely time to think, let alone spend time together.

Had he missed her?

Ever since their kiss the night of the Charity Ball, Zella couldn't seem to get Bert out of her mind, especially at night when she finally lay her head on the pillow. She dearly hoped he was similarly afflicted.

She unlocked the door to the department and turned up

the lamp. An icy chill clung to the air, so she chose not to remove her coat just yet. The janitor should be in shortly to turn up the radiators for the day.

In her office, the final copy for the typesetters was stacked neatly on her desk, tied with twine, and waiting to be delivered to the printer at ten. She and her sub-editor had spent the last two weeks combing through every word, checking for errors and, in a few cases, sending the original copy back to the writers to rewrite.

So why did she feel this urge to look through it one more time?

Opening her top drawer, Zella pulled out a pair of scissors. The twine popped when she snipped it. She laid aside the sheet of paper that said *Approved and Final, Forward Copy to Printer* in her slanted handwriting.

She skimmed through the first article on home décor and froze. Several misspelled words popped from the page.

She took a pencil from her drawer, marked the errors, and began carefully reading the entire stack of articles and editorials. Mistakes riddled the copy, page after page, from punctuation to laughable grammatical errors. One of her editorials, in which she'd spent a paragraph writing about the founding of Denwall, had the Walraven name spelled *Walravage*. Yet at the bottom of each page, her initials were as plain as day.

Had she really missed all these errors? Had her sub-editor?

It didn't matter, really, whose fault it was. The copy needed to be delivered to the typesetters in four hours if they were to stay on the production schedule.

She'd have to start typing up the new copy herself, since none of the assistants were due in the office until nine. Restacking the papers, Zella's mind whirled.

Don't panic. Still, her throat tightened.

She stood, then sat again when her head swam, and then stood once more.

Her office door creaked open. She inwardly winced as Bert stepped in, pushing his spectacles up his nose.

"You're here early," he said, but stopped short at the look on her face. "Something's wrong."

Her heart leaped at the sight of him, yet she despised how relieved she was. Like some weak female. "The final copy is due at the compositor this morning," she said quickly. "But I'm going to have to retype everything, and the printer won't hold up the press for me. They'll just move us to a later date, and we'll never get the book out on time."

Bert frowned. "Didn't you check the copy earlier? Why did you leave it until the last moment?"

So much for wanting him around. At that moment, she wanted to smash one of his eight-hundred-page tomes over his head. "Of course I checked it." Her words came out like a snap, but then she sighed and leaned against her desk. "I can't believe I overlooked so much. It's not like me at all." She hated it, but she was so close to tears, she didn't think she could stop them.

Bert pulled her into his arms, and she wept like a baby.

He handed her his handkerchief, and she blew her nose so hard it sounded like a trumpet. She caught the rumble of laughter in his chest.

What did she care if he laughed at her? Let him think she was uncouth. She was a failure of an editor-in-chief, and that was a pill more difficult to swallow.

When she stepped away from his embrace, he picked up the copy and read the first few pages. "I have a hard time believing these errors were in the copy you approved."

"They had to be. There's no other explanation."

He paced back and forth, his expression shifting from confusion to something sharper. "This isn't your fault. I think someone deliberately laid this stack on your desk, assuming you'd send it to the printer. Then, the mistakes wouldn't be found until you saw the galley proofs. Until it really was too late."

Zella's stomach roiled. To think that someone in the office hated her that much, that they'd go to the trouble of retyping over forty articles to add mistakes and make her look bad. It was like something out of a penny dreadful.

"Is this the first time someone has tried to undermine you?"

Zella stared. Before this moment, she hadn't connected any of the strange incidents but now he had her reconsidering events.

"I missed an important meeting a few weeks ago because of the wrong time written on my calendar. Misfiled paperwork is also a common occurrence and costs me valuable time to find it."

"Don't you file your own paperwork?"

"Yes, so I know where to find it!" She almost laughed at the irony but wiped a hand down her face and groaned. Should she tell him about the notes? What good would it do? They were childlike and silly. And typed. There was no way of knowing who wrote them.

More importantly, she didn't care to see the look on Bert's face when he read the lines that someone didn't think she was good enough to be here.

No, she'd hold that piece of information to herself for now. If another came, then she'd tell him.

Bert's eyes narrowed.

Zella saw the same tension in him that twisted inside her.

"I have to get this copy typed," she said finally.

"I'll help you. Give me half." Bert glanced at her desk clock. "My secretary will be in shortly, and we'll enlist her help as well. She's a very accurate typist. Then your assistants can finish it up when they get in."

Zella dipped her chin, her shoulders sagging with relief. "We might just make it."

"We will," he said, already loosening his cuffs and rolling up his sleeves. "But this isn't over, Zella. Whoever did this didn't count on you being thorough."

She managed a tight smile. "Or stubborn."

"Exactly. And we'll find them. But for now, let's prove them wrong."

Bert settled across from her at one of the gleaming type-writers in the production room. Soon, the rhythmic clack of typewriter keys echoed in the otherwise empty department. Zella found her resolve hardening. Someone wanted her to fail. But they had underestimated one crucial thing. She didn't stand alone.

⁘

Bypassing his usual seat at the far end of the room, Bert pulled out a chair next to Zella, who sat near the head of the board-room table, spine straight, expression composed but taut.

The call for a special meeting meant all of Denwall's top executives in the Philadelphia office were expected to attend. Even Father was there, although he declined Harlan's gesture for him to take his old seat at the head of the table.

Harlan cleared his throat. "I've called this meeting to discuss several disturbing events we should all be aware of and concerned about. Mrs. Capp has joined us today because of deliberate attempts to undermine *Denwall's European Styles Book*, one of our biggest projects in several years."

There were murmurs and a few startled frowns.

"To be clear," Harlan leaned forward and placed his fore-arms on the table, "these events have been perpetrated by one of our own employees who has access to a locked area. Make no mistake, this isn't just about the publications department. This kind of activity impacts all of us. Some of our competitors are not above bribing Denwall employees to spy on our business practices or even undermine our efforts."

Tom Morton leaned back in his chair. "That's what happens when you put a woman in charge of a big project. The company looks weak and vulnerable."

Of all the gall. Bert wished he could get Morton in a sparring ring. "It's tampering with documents and forgery. Could have happened to any of us."

James leaned forward, steepling his fingers on the table. "So it was altered after your approval, Mrs. Capp?"

"That's my assumption," she said. "We corrected and retyped everything before the deadline. The copy that went to the printer was accurate and clean."

James exhaled slowly. "You did well to catch it. I assume you're taking measures to prevent this in the future."

"I've implemented document security protocols," Zella said. "All future copy and illustrations are in a locked cabinet in my office, which will also remain locked if I'm not present. I've limited access to the final material to just three people."

Father cleared his throat, slow and deliberate. "When I said this project was ambitious, I didn't mean we should lose our heads or our oversight."

Zella shifted so that she faced him. "All in-house workers were hired before I arrived, Mr. Walraven. However, I take full responsibility for the actions of whoever is doing this and I intend to find out who they are."

The room fell silent.

Bert didn't miss the way Zella's shoulders squared, or the flicker of heat behind her calm tone. Not frantic. Not defensive. But angry, and that was far more effective.

After the meeting adjourned, Max caught him just outside their offices.

"Bert," he said quietly, "Between you and me, do you think we ought to bring in someone to help her manage this?"

Bert's jaw tightened. "No."

"It's a lot for one woman."

"She knows more about this magazine than any man in that room. If anything, we should be asking how she's managing everything with less-than-adequate staff and on a tight budget. A budget I forced her to adhere to."

Max held up his hands. "All right. I'm only asking."

"Mr. Dennison!" A voice called from the end of the hall. A stockroom employee, if Bert remembered correctly, hurried toward them, holding a package in his hands like it might catch fire.

The young man stopped in front of Max, breathless. "Found this in the garbage bin out by the street." He shrugged when Max narrowed his gaze. "Sometimes there's good stuff in the bins that my mother can use for the family."

Max took the brown paper package from the stockboy's outstretched hand. "It's not marked or labeled."

"No, sir, but I opened it and then rewrapped it. Go on, open it."

Bert moved in next to Max. As Max pulled back the wrapping to reveal the contents inside, Bert's heart hammered in his chest. "That's the copy Zella approved. The one that should have gone to the printer."

Max flipped through a few more pages and whistled. "So, this is the clean version? The one she swore she signed off on?"

"It is," Bert said. "And someone tossed it in the bin and replaced it with the retyped copy."

"What's your name, young man?" Max asked the stockboy.

"Henry, sir."

"You did the right thing, Henry. I appreciate you bringing

this to my attention. Would you do me a favor and please tell Mrs. Capp to come to my office?"

"Will do, sir." Henry puffed out his chest, then darted down the hall.

Max and Bert waited only five minutes for Zella to arrive, and they stood when she entered Max's office.

"You wanted to see me?"

Max pointed to the stack of papers on his desk. "This was found in the garbage bin outside."

"It's the original," Zella said as she flipped over a few of the pages. "The actual copy I approved."

Bert stood beside her, watching her face. She didn't look relieved, but furious.

"All that work to make sure this copy was perfect, to have it just thrown in the trash." She restacked the copy, her hands shaking. "Why would someone do this?"

The dejection on her face made Bert's chest ache. "Someone wants the publication to fail. Maybe they're targeting you specifically, I don't know. But they're getting sloppy." He glanced at Max. "We start watching everything. Every movement. Every document. If someone's trying to discredit Zella, we give them no room to succeed."

Max gave a quiet exhale. "Agreed."

After Zella left, Max turned to Bert. "Any idea who's behind all this?"

"Not yet, but I'll figure it out. And God help them when I do."

Nineteen

The stained-glass windows glowed like jewels in the morning light, casting rippling bands of color across the pews and polished floor. Zella sat alone in the back, her gloved hands folded in her lap.

She'd almost not come to church that morning, and she didn't want to attend St. Crispin's, where the Walravens and Dennisons would be. At the last moment she decided to try the smaller church not far from her apartment.

The week had been long and trying. The magazine was beginning its transition into layout and printing, and the pressure was mounting. She'd spent more nights at the Denwall offices than at her apartment, and her dreams—when she finally lay her head on her pillow—were a tangle of deadlines and doubts.

But this morning, something in her had whispered *go*.

So here she was. In a well-worn pew, trying not to look like she didn't belong.

The pastor, a tall, white-haired man with a gentle cadence and a slight rasp in his voice, stepped up to the pulpit,

"Today's passage," he said, opening his Bible, "is from

Isaiah. 'The Spirit of the Lord God is upon me; because the Lord hath anointed me to preach good tidings unto the meek; he hath sent me to bind up the brokenhearted, to proclaim liberty to the captives, and the opening of the prison to them that are bound.'"

Zella's stomach clenched. Often, after Da had had a particularly bad day and took it out on her and Mam, Mam would say that God lifted the brokenhearted and the beaten down. By the time Zella left the farm, she no longer believed the sentiment.

"We don't often like to admit when we're brokenhearted," the pastor continued. "Even less when we feel crushed. We're proud creatures. Capable. Resilient. Especially those of us who've been told we have to be."

Zella's fingers tightened slightly.

"But God doesn't measure worth by resilience. He doesn't wait for us to come to Him strong. He comes close when we're beaten down. He draws near when we're unsure of our own value. And He sets us free."

She'd tried to fight the pressing feeling that the anonymous notes caused. Yet the cruel words of someone who didn't deserve a second thought remained tucked in her heart.

You're not good enough.

She'd tried to push past it, to dismiss it as cowardly, petty. But it had burrowed into her all the same. Because a part of her had always believed it. Her father had told her so many times.

On the outside, she could fight back with sharp words and self-discipline and late nights. She could present polished ideas, elegant layouts, and witty retorts. But inside? She was tired of having to prove she was worthy of respect.

And now, this pastor says God doesn't require her to be polished or certain. *What do I do with that?*

The choir began a soft refrain behind the pastor's closing

prayer. Zella closed her eyes. She didn't know if she believed the words spoken in this place. But she wanted to. She wanted to believe she wasn't alone—that someone drew near, understood the weight she carried, and didn't ask her to carry it alone.

Zella joined the congregation in song, and later, when she stepped into the cold light of the morning, she stopped and stared at the gray sky. Something told her she must stop hiding behind a trumped-up persona. That she needed to reveal the unvarnished truth that was Zella Abbott Capp.

She turned to go, pulling her gloves on, when a voice stopped her.

"Madam?"

Zella looked up to find the pastor standing just inside the vestibule.

"I wanted to thank you for coming today," he said. "I know it can take a little courage to walk into a place like this when you don't know anyone. But this is the best place to come when you're carrying a heavy burden."

Zella offered a wary smile. "I wasn't aware it showed."

He gave a soft chuckle. "It always does, but few will admit it." There was a pause, but then he added, "You're welcome back anytime. Doesn't have to be a Sunday. You can slip into one of our pews and sit in silence without having to explain. Or, if you ever want to talk, I'm usually in my office on Mondays and Thursdays. You're always welcome here."

Zella nodded, not trusting her voice. "Thank you, Pastor."

He inclined his head, and she stepped into the bright light of day.

Zella stirred the pot of tea twice clockwise, once counterclockwise. It was a habit she'd picked up from Florence. Funny that after being together for so long, their habits became similar. Probably not unlike a married couple.

The steam curled toward her cheek, and she took a sip. Outside her apartment window, the sun had yet to make an appearance over the city.

She'd leave for work as soon as it was light. Until then, she had two letters to write—one to Florence and one to Ivy.

She hadn't heard from Florence in weeks.

That in itself wasn't cause for panic. Florence Ashford wasn't one for frequent correspondence. Still, something gnawed at Zella. The last letter had arrived in early January, full of her usual dry wit and complaints about Quentin's latest schemes. Florence had signed it with her signature, *As ever, F.A.*

But that was six weeks ago.

Zella carried the tea to her rolltop desk, set it down, and reached for several sheets of writing paper.

Dearest Florence,

The magazine is nearing press, and I finally believe it might be real. That it might be something worth keeping. I wonder if you'd laugh or just nod in that knowing way of yours, as if I'd only just caught up to what you already believed.

How are you faring? Have you seen the doctor again? I wish you would write. Just a line would do.

Zella stared at the ink blot that formed when she'd paused too long. Her throat tightened.

She hadn't allowed herself to feel it—that edge of helplessness, of not knowing, of being too far away to do anything. Florence had been more than a former employer. She'd been a guardian. A conspirator. A confidante.

And now, Zella couldn't shake the feeling that something was wrong.

She finished the short letter, folded it, and tucked it into an addressed envelope. She took another fortifying sip of tea, then pushed her teacup aside and stood.

The apartment felt too quiet. The kind of quiet she used to crave.

Moving to the window, she leaned her head against the cold pane. Without thinking, she whispered, "Lord, please let her be all right. Please allow me the trip we've planned for April. I need to see her. To be with her. To make sure she's being cared for properly." The prayer wasn't elegant, nor was it long. But it was more prayer than she'd offered in years. And saying it out loud made something in her ache.

She covered her face with her hands. *I don't know what to do if something were to happen to her.* For the second time in less than two weeks, unwanted tears fell.

Enough. Crying never solved anything. Having no handkerchief nearby, Zella dabbed at her cheeks with her sleeve and crossed to her desk. She sat in the straight back chair and dipped her pen into the inkpot once more. She had one more letter to write and send today.

My Dearest Ivy,

I've tried writing this letter many times, only to discard each attempt. This one must reach you because I no longer can bear the weight of silence. You are the truest friend I have, and I trust you above all others with this confession.

I have deceived everyone around me, including you, and for that, I am deeply sorry. I hope you will come to understand the motives behind my deception.

My truth, unvarnished, is that there was never a Jeremiah Capp who died and left me a widow. I've never been married. Florence Ashford and your mother were the only ones who knew my secret. Now one is gone, and the other is fading, I'm afraid.

When I first spun this story, I thought it would grant me independence and freedom from society's judgment. I wanted to build a life where I wasn't pressured into a marriage I did not want. I also wanted to write articles that magazines would publish. Adjusting my history to that of a widow seemed the simplest way to accomplish both goals. I know my motives sound selfish, and I don't deny that they were.

Now, however, it's time to end the lie, no matter the consequences. I no longer want to spend the rest of my life alone, but that means I'll need to move forward in truth.

Zella stopped and stared out her apartment window. Rain fell against the pane, hard enough that the scene outside blurred.

Certainly, she'd have to tell *everyone* the truth as soon as she finished the Denwall project. For her own peace of mind, it couldn't wait any longer. They'd want nothing else to do with her, no doubt. She dreaded the disappointment she'd surely see in Bert's eyes. But she couldn't keep deceiving someone she loved.

Love.

Yes, she loved Bert Walraven, as crazy as that sounded. Her heart had known the truth the moment they kissed on the balcony at the Academy of Music. Her brain had taken longer to accept it, however.

They say opposites attract, and she and Bert were as different as satin and fur.

Zella shook her head. It didn't matter. He'd never forgive her.

I tell you first, Ivy, because I owe you this truth most of all. I will be in New York for your wedding in April, if you still want me there, and we can speak face-to-face. Perhaps by then, I will have the courage to tell everyone, and a direction for rebuilding my life.

Please forgive me for this burden I've placed on you. Know that I love you dearly and hope you can find it in your heart to forgive me.

Your loving aunt, Zella

With a deep sigh, Zella folded the letter carefully, slipped it into an envelope, and sealed it swiftly before doubt could again sway her mind. Rising from her desk, she placed the letter in her reticule and glanced at the clock.

She'd mail the letters this evening. Right now, she needed to get to work.

Am I procrastinating again?

Most definitely.

Twenty

※

"Mrs. Capp?" Zella's sub-editor hovered in her office doorway with a folder in hand and a wide grin on his face.

"Yes?"

"I just wanted to let you know that sales signed off on the final product descriptions." He stepped inside and held out the folder. "Also, the new cover proofs arrived from the printer. They're spectacular."

Zella accepted the folder and gave the young man a tired smile. "You've been a marvel this week, Mr. Smith. Thank you."

There was a beat, and he shuffled his feet. "We'll make the deadline, won't we?"

"We will," Zella said firmly. "We've come too far to fail now."

Mr. Smith gave her a quick tip of his head and strode back to his desk. Zella glanced at her calendar. Twenty more days until Denwall distributed the magazine. A little over six weeks until the wedding, when she'd need the courage to look at Ivy face-to-face.

During her weakest moments, she regretted being hasty with the confession she'd mailed to Ivy two days before.

Should she have waited until after Ivy and Will's wedding? Maybe. But something told her that they needed to start their new life together without a family secret waiting in the wings that could hurt them both.

Truth be told, her reason for telling Ivy was purely selfish. Zella just couldn't live with it any longer. Love did that to a person, she guessed. Once she had the chance to make amends to Ivy in person, then she'd tell Bert. Still, it was a big assumption on her part that Ivy wouldn't tell Will. Of course she would. But hopefully, he'd allow Zella to explain the deception to his family herself when she felt the time was right.

She didn't look up when a knock sounded at her door but continued writing notes in the margins of the galley proofs. Her staff knew she didn't stand on ceremony.

"Come in."

The door creaked open and closed far too precisely, causing Zella to look up from her desk.

Alva Holcroft? Zella hadn't seen her since the Charity Ball. What was she doing at Denwall?

"Mrs. Holcroft," she said, schooling her expression into polite neutrality. "This is a surprise."

"Most worthwhile visits are." The woman's overpowering perfume filled the small office as she stepped closer. "I happened to be in the neighborhood and thought I'd offer a word of caution."

"Caution?"

"About your, shall we say, reputation?" Mrs. Holcroft's tone was cool, her smile smug. "One must be ever so careful when climbing into society's good graces. Such heights, after all, make any tumble quite the spectacle."

Zella set her pencil down, spine straight. "I have no idea what you're talking about."

Mrs. Holcroft gave a soft tsk. "Come, now, *Mrs.* Capp. Must we play the innocent? A widow, are you? How tragic." She plucked a typewritten note from her reticule. "Someone sent me an illuminating piece of information about your sweet confession to your niece in New York. Another undeserving social climber."

Zella's hands turned clammy, and she felt the blood drain from her face.

"How did you—?" Had Ivy told Will, and then Will told this woman?

No, that didn't make any sense.

"You left your office unlocked, dear. Such a careless habit for someone with so much to hide."

Someone had gone through her reticule and found the letter to Ivy before she had the chance to mail it.

Stupid, stupid, stupid. She knew there was someone out to ruin her. Knew she needed to keep everything under lock and key. Which she did in a cabinet behind her desk. She just didn't think of her personal items, like her reticule.

Zella stood slowly. "That letter's contents were private and the envelope sealed."

"And yet those contents found their way to me. You see, secrets are terrible at staying hidden. Especially when they involve fabricated husbands." She clicked her tongue. "A shame, really. You've done rather well for someone of your background."

Zella swallowed the fury rising in her throat. "What do you want?"

"Oh, nothing dramatic." Mrs. Holcroft waved a gloved hand. "I simply need a small influx of cash. My husband's generosity has waned lately, and one grows tired of begging for every new gown or bauble."

"You want money?" Zella's laugh was brittle. "I'm not wealthy."

"Oh, come now. I'm certain you make a nice wage here at Denwall. At the very least, you know people you can borrow from."

Zella stiffened. "How much do you want?"

Mrs. Holcroft waved a long-fingered hand. "Two hundred should cover my immediate needs. And in return, I'll stay silent. You keep your little job and your fake reputation. Everybody wins."

Two hundred was more than Zella made in two months. Her voice came out low, but steady. "No."

"I beg your pardon?"

"You heard me. I won't be bribed. Besides, I planned to make my marriage status public anyway."

Mrs. Holcroft leaned forward, her perfume a choking cloud of violets. "But not until after your niece's wedding in April."

True. "Doesn't matter. I still won't play your game."

"Then prepare yourself for the scandal you so desperately wanted to avoid."

"Do what you must." Zella wouldn't let this horrible woman see her flinch.

Mrs. Holcroft narrowed her eyes, then pivoted on her heel. "So be it. But when your precious magazine crashes before it's published and you fall from favor with the Walravens and Dennisons, remember you had a choice." She swept from the room.

Zella sat down before her wobbly legs buckled. She had no doubt that Mrs. Holcroft's next stop would be Harlan's office.

The click of Mrs. Holcroft's shoes echoed down the hallway,

but her words lingered in Bert's office like the smoke from a cheap cigar.

When his secretary had announced her arrival ten minutes before, he'd assumed Mrs. Holcroft wanted money from Denwall for some charity event or another.

He couldn't have been more mistaken. Instead, she landed a punch he'd not expected.

Zella wasn't Mrs. Zella Capp. Never had been.

Bert wandered to the window and gazed out at the street below.

How could she lie for so long? And, apparently, she'd lied to everyone, including Ivy, if what Mrs. Holcroft said was true.

He turned back to his desk to find Zella standing outside the doorway to his office.

She didn't say anything.

Neither did he.

She looked like she might, though—like she had a dozen words half-formed behind her lips, explanations crowding against apology. But Bert shook his head once and walked out the door.

He brushed past her, not looking her in the face.

He didn't slam his door. Didn't raise his voice. But he couldn't talk with her right now. Not until he'd sorted the snarl of thoughts unraveling in his chest.

She lied.

To her family. To the company. *To me.*

He crossed the corridor and rang the bell for the elevator. Once it arrived, he slipped in and waited for the elevator operator to close the door.

He clenched his fists and squeezed his eyes shut.

Zella. Sharp. Brilliant. Composed. He had trusted her instincts. Defended her in board meetings. Watched her lead, push, charm, and deliver. And all this time, she had built it on a lie. A deception she perpetrated for years. Long before they met, of course, but that thought didn't untangle the knot behind his ribs.

When he reached the main floor, he stepped out of the elevator and ran into Max, who took one look at Bert and winced. "You look like you've been hit by a trolley."

Bert didn't smile. "Where're you headed?"

"To see Zella. Thought we had a quick note to review on the next layout. Strange, but I ran into Alva Holcroft a minute ago. What was she doing here?"

"She came to give me some news."

Max raised a brow. "That's cryptic. Even for you."

"She implied," Bert stopped and blew out a breath, "no, she stated that Zella was never married. That her whole story about being a widow—her married name—it was all a fabrication. Somehow, Alva heard about a letter Zella had written to Ivy. A confession of sorts."

Max let out a low whistle.

"Zella told me nothing," Bert said. "And I—" His heart splintered. "I kissed her."

"You say that like it was a crime."

"I don't—" Bert ran a hand through his hair. "I don't know what it was. But I thought I knew her."

Max folded his arms. "You still might." When Bert shot him a look but said nothing, Max shrugged. "People hide things for all sorts of reasons. Myra used to say that society isn't kind to women with no husband and too many opinions. Zella has both."

"She lied."

"She survived," Max said. "You've seen how she works. How she carries herself. Do you really believe she's dishonest? Or do you just feel betrayed that she didn't pick you to confess it to first?"

That landed hard, but Bert said nothing.

Max gave him a more thoughtful look. "You've always

been good at numbers, Bert. Calculations. But you and I both know life doesn't line up into nice, neat columns."

"No. But I can't abide liars."

"Did you ask for her side of the story?"

Bert shrugged. "No."

"And don't you think Ivy, of all people, had the right to know first? Maybe Zella planned to tell you, too, but Alva beat her to it."

"Maybe."

Max narrowed his eyes. "This begs another question. How did Alva find out?"

"She said someone had read Zella's letter of confession to Ivy. It was in her reticule to be mailed, I gather."

Max poked his finger at Bert's chest. "So someone has yet again undermined Zella. Someone at Denwall." When Bert inclined his head, Max continued. "We need to figure out who, and soon."

Yes, they did. And Bert needed to talk to Zella.

Twenty-One

Zella returned to her office and stared at the work on her desk that she couldn't seem to focus on.

Bert's reaction to the news that she wasn't a widow didn't surprise her. For the first time in her life, she hadn't been able to summon a clever line or a retort to break the silence he left behind.

She felt like a woman twice her age. Her heart ached. Her pride burned. But beneath it all was a deep and unmistakable grief.

You waited too long.

She opened the top drawer, pulled out a sheet of Denwall letterhead, and wrote her resignation in neat, deliberate script. Not because she wanted to. But because it felt like the only honorable thing left to do. She'd give them the chance to find someone to take her place if they even wanted her around that long.

Zella folded the letter, pressed it flat, and slipped it into her dress pocket. She started to walk around her desk when Bert appeared at the door.

"Hello, Bert." The quiet greeting was all she could manage.

"Zella." He stepped inside and closed the door behind him.

"I sent a letter to Ivy," she said, before he could speak. "Two days ago. I told her I wasn't a widow. That I'd made the marriage up, and that I planned to tell you and your family after her wedding. I left it in my purse to mail after work. I don't know how Alva got hold of the information."

He didn't speak, didn't move. Just waited. She pulled the letter to James and Harlan out of her pocket.

"I've written my resignation. I was just about to go upstairs to hand it in."

"Isn't that a little rash?" The question wasn't exactly gentle. "You still need to finish the *Styles Book*."

Zella's legs wobbled, and she found she could no longer stand. Thank goodness her chair was handy. "I'll stay and finish it. I want to finish it. But I'm also giving Denwall the chance to cut me loose before there's a scandal."

Bert shook his head and folded his tall frame into the chair in front of her desk.

For a few seconds, he didn't speak. Just stared at her. "Why didn't you tell anyone who you were long before now?"

She straightened her shoulders. "I told my friend Florence and my sister, but I asked them to never tell a soul. I was afraid it would undo everything I'd worked toward."

"It did," he said quietly, and she flinched. "Not the magazine," he added, more measured now. "Not your work. At least I don't think so. Just the part where I thought I knew you."

She let out a breath, sharp and shaky. "I didn't make up a husband to deceive you or anyone. I did it because no one listens to a woman alone. Especially not in the places I needed to be."

"You could've built a reputation eventually."

"I didn't have time," she said. "I had no connections. Not much money. And I had two choices, pretend to be a married woman who'd lost her husband, and hope someone would hire me to write for them, or go back to Ohio and marry a farmer three times my age who wanted a cook and a broodmare."

Bert looked away.

"I'm so sorry." Her words came out in a whisper.

Bert stood. "So am I." And he walked out the door.

Zella blinked back the tears, stunned at how cold his words felt.

"No sense crying over spilled milk," she muttered to herself. She squared her shoulders and strode out of her office. All eyes in the publications department were on her, but she said nothing and headed straight to the executive wing.

She found James in his office, sitting at his desk, reading spectacles perched on the top of his nose.

"Mr. Dennison," she said, drawing the folded letter from her pocket. "This is my formal resignation."

He looked up, brows lifting. "Good heavens. Sit down."

She hesitated, then sank into the chair opposite his desk.

James's eyes skimmed the letter. He removed his spectacles, his eyes now searching her face. "I assume this is about the rumor flying around the building? The one about you not really being a widow?"

"It's true. I never married. I concocted the story and the name years ago. For safety. For respectability. I never imagined I'd still be carrying it."

"I've raised four daughters," he said in a kind voice, setting the letter on his desk. "I know the obstacles women face. I know why you did it. It was wrong, perhaps, but not malicious. And if I had to wager, I'd guess most women in our readership would understand exactly why you did it."

Zella's heart thudded. "What are you saying?"

"I'm saying let's not be hasty. Let me speak to the board. I'd like to suggest to them that we use this opportunity." He leaned forward. "What if, instead of hiding this, you wrote about it?"

She stared at him.

"A piece for the magazine," he continued. "Deflect the possible scandal."

"An article titled 'Why I Pretended to Be a Widow' perhaps." She tapped her fingers on the arm of her chair.

"There you go. You'd be surprised how many women would thank you for it."

Zella exhaled, something loosening in her chest. James wasn't letting her off the hook. But he wasn't throwing her overboard, either. "If that's what you'd like."

"Good," he said. "I'll personally ask the few who overheard not to spread it further, and I'll speak to Alva Holcroft's husband about his wife's meddling. It buys us time."

She nodded slowly, rising to her feet.

As she reached the door, he added, "And Zella? Remember that the Lord forgives." His voice was calm, almost fatherly. "Not because we've earned it, but because Christ already paid the price."

Zella didn't speak, afraid she would break down on the threshold of James's door.

She didn't return to her office right away but went outside where the sun was shining and spring was hinting at an early arrival. She walked across the street to a park, sat on a bench, and closed her eyes against the brightness.

She had lied. She had failed. And yet she was forgiven. *Not because I've earned it...*

The wind stirred the leaves at her feet, and she bowed her head.

She whispered a prayer—not eloquent or polished, just

honest. For forgiveness. For strength. For wisdom. For the courage to stand in the light instead of hiding in the shadows of an untruth.

And for a way forward she couldn't yet see.

Laura Walraven had just set down her embroidery when she heard the front door open. They were two weeks into Lent, so this was no social visit. Most people were taking a pause from the season's whirl until after Easter.

She was grateful for the time that would allow her to heal and help Caroline finish her season. Not that Zella hadn't done an excellent job. She had. But a daughter's first season was a watershed event, and Laura wanted to cry at the thought of all the gatherings she'd missed over the past three months.

The sound of heavy footfalls in the hallway outside meant it was probably Bert. Ned was at school and Charles was in his study, so it only made sense that the visitor was her eldest.

She smoothed her hair from her face and rang the bell for one of the maids to bring in a pot of tea and cookies.

Bert paused just outside the parlor doorway, but then entered the room, his hair windblown and his collar stretched. He looked like he'd come in from a storm. Or brought one with him.

Ever since New York, when he was ambushed in the park and left for dead, he hadn't been the same. He appeared untethered, like a rowboat on a rocky ocean.

He bent and kissed her cheek. "Hello, Mother. How are you faring? Your color's good, you must be feeling better." He chattered on like a magpie, about the weather, the state of the roads, and the tulips beginning to grow in the front garden.

Tulips?

"You seem restless," Laura said lightly, watching him pace to the hearth and back again.

He rubbed a hand along the back of his neck. "I guess I am a bit. Just needed to think. Figured the walk would help, and I ended up here."

"It's a nice day out. Do you feel better now?"

He gave her a wan smile. "Not particularly."

When he finally stopped to take a breath, she narrowed her gaze at his reddened knuckles.

"You've been at the gym again. Don't bother denying it."

Behind his spectacles, Bert's eyes opened and closed like an owl's. "How did you know?"

"I carried you in my arms, dear. You think I wouldn't notice when you come here smelling faintly of liniment? And your knuckles are bruised and scraped."

His half-smile was sheepish, but tired. "I go there with Max every so often."

"I think it's more than that, but never mind. I understand." She motioned to the settee. "Sit. I just rang for tea."

He settled in with a sigh that came from somewhere deep in his chest.

Laura watched him for a moment in silence. The boy who'd once brought her squashed violets and bruised knees now sat with a weight on his shoulders that she didn't know how to lift.

"I take it something happened," she said gently.

He didn't answer right away. Instead, he braced his forearms on his thighs, staring down at the floor. "Do you remember that world globe Father used to keep in his study?"

"Of course."

"He used to spin it when he was upset. Said it helped him remember how small we all were in the grand scheme." He exhaled. "I feel like someone's been spinning me."

She waited. Mothers were good at that. A maid came

through with tea and cookies, and Laura poured Bert a cup the way he liked it. Very sweet.

Finally, he spoke, "Zella lied."

Ah. There it was. Laura took a slow sip of her tea before asking, "About what?"

"She's not a widow. Never was. Made the whole thing up years ago."

Laura didn't allow her face to show any surprise at this news. She simply set her cup down and folded her hands. "And you only just found out?"

"Today." His jaw worked for a second. "From someone else. I think she was planning to tell me, but—"

"But someone got there first. And it hurt."

He frowned, but she continued, her voice soft. "You wouldn't be here if it didn't."

He sat back and stared at the fire for a long moment.

"I don't understand why she did it," he said. "She's smart. Talented. More than capable."

"Did she give you an explanation?"

"I gather her father was overbearing. Threatened to marry her off to an Ohio farmer old enough to be her grandfather. She ran away from home."

"I assume she was a young woman alone, with probably no money," Laura said. "And if her father was abusive, the idea of marrying for convenience's sake was probably repulsive to her. So she did what she could to better herself and build a career. But you know as well as I do that the world doesn't offer many safe lanes for a woman like her to run in."

Bert was quiet, but she knew her son, and the turning wheels in his head almost caused smoke to come out of his ears.

"The Bible says the Lord sees not as man sees. We look at the outward appearance, but the Lord looks on the heart."

"Yes, I'm familiar with the passage."

"Sweetheart, I don't condone deception. But there's more to Zella than the façade she's lived under. And I know your heart. You wouldn't be this angry if you didn't already care more than you meant to."

He looked at his reddened and bruised hands.

"And you saw her for who she is inside. That doesn't disappear because of one untruth. Especially one born from necessity, not malice." She reached over and squeezed his hand. "You're your father's son, but you're also mine. Like me, you know when something is worth holding on to, even when it's uncomfortable."

Bert wiped a hand down his face. "What do I do?"

"You give it time. You ask the Lord to help you separate your pride from your principles. And if what you saw in her is still there, you forgive."

He nodded slowly.

She didn't press him. Didn't tell him to stop boxing. She'd let him keep his outlet—for now.

But she prayed silently, as mothers do, that one day he'd find his refuge in love and not fists.

TWENTY-TWO

Zella took a hansom cab from her apartment to the Walton Hotel on Broad and Locust. She'd accepted an invitation from Myra and Lena for a Saturday luncheon *to get her out in public*, as Myra put it.

Ever since the debacle with Alva Holcroft, she'd kept a low profile, which wasn't difficult because she'd been very busy at work. They were down to the last three weeks before Easter and the launch of the *Styles Book*.

It had been four weeks since she'd dropped the last name Capp and stepped into her new identity as Miss Abbott, spinster. She didn't mind that so much, and James and Harlan were extremely supportive, considering.

A week after she sent her letter to Ivy, she received a return note. Short and to the point, Ivy wrote that she understood why Zella had done what she had. She couldn't understand keeping it from her, however. Zella prayed that once she was back in New York, they could mend fences.

Bert was a different story. Although he wasn't rude or dismissive, whatever warmth was there before had vanished. Only a professional relationship remained. For that, more than anything that had transpired, Zella had the deepest regret.

He'd been in New York for the better part of three weeks, and they hadn't exchanged more than a few words before he left.

Would he ever forgive her?

That thought haunted her. Not in her dreams—she didn't sleep deeply anymore, so they didn't come—but in the stillness between thoughts. The quiet moments when she stopped moving long enough to feel the ache in her chest.

She missed him. Missed the way his quiet steadiness filled a room. Missed the way she could feel him watching her when he thought she didn't realize it. Missed his quick wit and the way he challenged her.

Yes, she missed him. More than she ever thought she could miss another human being, let alone a man.

Zella paused beneath the grand marble stairway of the newly opened Hotel Walton, just long enough to absorb the lobby's magnificence. Light poured through the stained-glass skylight far above, striking the ivory-toned panels and glinting off the polished bronze moldings. A marble balustrade circled the mezzanine.

"Zella!" Myra Dennison waved from beside a uniformed attendant. "They've already seated us in the Palm Café."

Zella gathered her skirts, passed through the grand archway to her right, and followed Myra and Lena toward the restaurant. She'd seen photographs of the new hotel in *The Inquirer*, but none had prepared her for the overwhelming splendor.

The Palm Café was tucked to the east of the grand lobby. In the Venetian Gothic style, the walls were a rich Tuscan red and paneled in eight-foot-high wainscotting. True to its name, dozens of palms and evergreens bedecked the room.

Their table stood near one of the windows, framed in

thick drapery. A waiter pulled out chairs with discreet grace, nodding to each lady in turn.

"I've heard they imported the tile from Tunis," Lena said, smoothing the cuffs of her lemon-colored jacket. "And the fixtures were cast in Vienna. I read the architect studied in Paris."

Zella appreciated the Dennisons' attempts to steer clear of the reason they probably invited her to lunch. They wanted to provide her with support out in public. Despite James's best efforts at keeping the employees of Denwall quiet about her married or *unmarried* status, he couldn't stop Alva Holcroft from spreading the gossip in polite society faster than a wildfire in a dry forest. No one in the publications department said a word, but conversation stopped when she passed by, and her office had become her refuge.

The waiter returned with menus printed on vellum, and Zella's eyes wandered once more over the room's detailing, from electric lights in gilded sconces, to the marble floor that gleamed like still water.

Zella was trying to enjoy her tea when the whispering began.

It started at the far end of the café in a cluster of Philadelphia matrons seated beneath the enormous wall mirror. Their glances kept drifting in her direction, lips pressed into disapproving lines as they exchanged quiet words behind gloved hands.

Her back straight, Zella curled her fingers around her teacup. On either side of her, Lena and Myra continued their conversation, seemingly unaffected.

But Zella felt it. That old, familiar sensation of being weighed, measured, and found lacking.

"They've been like that since we walked in," Lena murmured.

"Like crows over a carcass," Myra added, not bothering to

lower her voice. She sliced a roll in half with a butter knife, as if imagining a more satisfying target.

Zella shrugged her stiff shoulders. "Maybe they're just wondering why I'm here."

"Let them wonder," Myra said. "They haven't had anything interesting to whisper about since Beatrice Pomeroy's second husband *accidentally* fell into their front yard fountain."

One woman across the room, Mrs. Prudence Langley of the Charity Ball Committee, rose and made a deliberate path toward their table.

"Oh no," Zella muttered.

"Stay seated," Myra said coolly. "I'll deal with her."

Prudence reached the edge of their table and offered a sugar-sweet smile that did nothing to soften the ice behind her eyes. "Miss Abbott," she said in a tone that was both greeting and accusation. "How very brave of you to come here."

Zella tilted her head. "Brave?"

"Well, with everything that's come to light, it's simply admirable that you would continue to show yourself in public."

Lena stiffened. Myra's teacup hit the saucer with a decisive clink.

Zella straightened her shoulders. If this self-important woman thought she could make her cower, she had another think coming. "I wasn't aware dining at a public establishment required patrons to be without fault."

"Maybe not, but we expect to dine next to people of upstanding character, not gutter snipes."

Myra stood. The entire tearoom seemed to hush.

"Prudence," Myra said with a dangerous smile, "you seem to have mistaken this establishment for a pulpit. If you're quite finished with your sermon, I suggest you return to your tea before I unleash some interesting truths about *you*."

Prudence's lips thinned. "I only meant—"

"What you meant," Myra said, "was to humiliate a woman for doing what society all but demands—survive alone, or attach herself to a name that keeps the wolves at bay. If that makes you uncomfortable, I suggest examining the bars of your own gilded cage."

Gasps followed like a wave through the room.

Prudence pointed a long finger at Myra. "Don't threaten me, Myra Dennison. You don't do Miss Abbott any favors by being her friend. You're an outcast. No one would believe anything you say." Her cheeks flushed nearly as red as the strawberries on the table centerpiece.

Zella sucked in a breath and opened her mouth to respond but caught two figures she hadn't seen earlier walking through the restaurant and heading their way.

Bert and Max. They must have eaten lunch and were on their way out. Had they overheard her conversation with Prudence?

"Ladies." Max tipped his head when they reached the table. "And Mrs. Langley."

Zella almost snorted at the well-placed insult.

"Is everything all right here, Miss Abbott?" Bert asked, his voice like steel. He put a warm hand on her shoulder in a show of solidarity and shifted his eyes to Prudence. "Is there a problem, Mrs. Langley?"

"Well," she sputtered, "I'm just questioning whether this is the best place for Miss Abbott to dine."

"I would think it's the perfect place for her to be. In fact, she's probably better than this place deserves, if you are any indication of its clientele."

Prudence's eyes bugged out of her face. "Well, I never! My husband will hear about this! He's an investor in Denwall, you know."

"And as an investor, I'm sure he wouldn't appreciate

knowing you are insulting a managing director of the company. In public. A highly respected director, I might add."

Prudence turned on her heel and marched back to her table. Instead of sitting again with her companions, she picked up her reticule and left the restaurant.

"Thank you, Bert," Zella said quietly.

Bert inclined his head and walked away.

He may have defended her, but he still hadn't forgiven her.

Bert took a deep breath as he stepped outside the Walton Hotel. The spring air held the tang of early blossoms and a trace of coal smoke. Carriages rattled down the avenue, but he barely registered them.

Max strode beside him, unusually quiet for about ten seconds—a personal best. "I don't know whether to applaud you or invite you to a match in the ring just so I can take a swing at you."

Bert stopped mid-stride on the sidewalk and turned to glare at his friend. Someone he'd grown up with. Trusted. Knew like a brother. At least he thought he did. "What are you blathering about? Why would you want to hit me? I defended her, didn't I?" He resumed his march toward home, regretting accepting Max's invitation to lunch with every step.

Max caught up easily. "Yes, you defended her. That's the part I applaud. But you also walked away. And after everything Zella's been through, that must have felt a lot like abandonment."

Bert's jaw tightened. Speaking of punching, he'd like to knock that calm expression off Max's face. "I didn't snub Zella. I just had nothing else to say."

Even to his own ears, it sounded like a weak excuse.

Max didn't rub it in. He just walked beside him, letting the silence thicken.

Bert exhaled. "I shouldn't have interfered back there."

"If you hadn't, I would have."

"I'm afraid I just made it worse."

"You think standing up for her made it worse?"

"No," Bert said, pausing beneath a row of spindly trees outside his townhouse. "But touching her shoulder like that, standing beside her—what was I trying to say? That everything's fine? That I'm laying claim to her? I'm not."

Max looked him square in the eye. "It didn't look like a claim, but more like someone protecting a colleague who was being bullied. A decent man refusing to let cruelty stand."

Bert opened his front door and stepped inside. His housekeeper had weekends off, and the house sat in lonely stillness. There was no fire lit, no clatter from the kitchen. Just the tick of the hall clock.

He tossed his hat onto the foyer table and rubbed the back of his neck. "I don't know what else I can do. I wrestled with it, prayed about it, and finally came to understand why she didn't tell me the truth sooner. I got to the other side of resentment."

He walked into the parlor and dropped into his favorite armchair. "But now I'm stuck in this no-man's-land. I don't know what comes next."

Max followed, sat on the settee, and tugged off his boots. "You mean you don't know if *she* wants anything to come next." He swung his legs up on the velvet cushions.

"Make yourself at home," Bert grumbled.

Max grinned. "I always do." He stared at the ceiling for a few seconds and then returned his blue eyes to Bert's face. "You know, you've always kept strict control of your life. Your career, your reputation, even your emotions. But I've noticed something since New York."

Bert didn't like the direction of Max's thoughts. Not one bit. "What about New York?"

"Since the mugging," Max said simply. "You've been different. Not just the boxing. You've been tenser. Like you've doubled down on trying to keep everything in check. As if you just plan hard enough, prepare enough, you'll never get blindsided again."

Bert leaned back in the chair. "You're quite the psychoanalyst. Should I pay you for your time?"

"The advice is free for a friend," Max said with a chuckle. "And look, I understand. The mugging scared you. It should have. But somewhere along the line, you didn't just start fighting back physically, you also started closing yourself off emotionally. You want to control who gets close, how close, when, and why. Because if you're in control, you think you can't get hurt."

Bert gave a hollow laugh. "Amazing. You got all that from my trips to the gym."

"You've always liked things to add up. Maybe that's why you're an excellent numbers man. But maybe it's time to stop being a financial director with your heart."

Bert rubbed a hand down his face. His head was starting to pound. "I'm open to a relationship."

"With someone who won't ask anything messy of you? Maybe. But Zella? She's not neat. Not easy. She's not a column that can be reconciled. And that terrifies you."

"It doesn't terrify me," Bert said too quickly.

Max arched a brow. "Really? Because from where I'm sitting, you've forgiven her with your head, but not your heart. You've let go of the grudge but not the control."

Bert stared at the plush rug beneath his feet.

"You've already done the easy part," Max said gently. "Now comes the difficult step."

Bert sighed. "Let me guess. Letting myself *want more.*"

"Exactly."

"I don't even know her plans." Bert shifted restlessly, adjusting the cuff of his sleeve. "After the *Styles Book* launches, she's leaving. Going back to New York."

"Then give her a reason to stay."

Bert looked at him, startled.

"You know what I saw in that café?" Max continued. "A woman trying to hold her head high while people whispered behind her back. And then I saw her breathe again when you walked up. Like someone just handed her a life preserver in the middle of a storm."

"That's a generous interpretation."

"It's what happened. And you don't have to take my word for it—you just have to ask yourself what she means to you. And if she still means something to you, Bert, then you need to tell her. Not tomorrow. Not in a business memo. *Now*. Before someone else decides your story for you."

The words hung in the air between them like smoke.

"Thanks for the advice. I'll think about it."

Max swung his legs over the side of the settee and stood. "Make sure you don't think too long."

Twenty-Three

Zella stirred a pot of carrot soup with one hand while reading over printer proofs with the other. The meal wasn't glamorous, but it was nourishing and easy to eat standing up. Her days had become a blur of fast meals, late nights, and endless final adjustments.

The print run would start tomorrow. If all went according to plan, the *Styles Book* would finish rolling off the presses just in time for distribution the first Monday after Easter. They were on schedule. On budget. On the cusp of something truly extraordinary.

She should've felt triumphant.

Instead, she felt hollow.

The apartment was warm, quiet, filled with the soft tick of the clock and the subtle scent of coriander and roasted carrots. But none of it settled her. None of it felt like victory.

Because it wasn't enough. Not anymore.

A week ago, the letter from *Pall Mall Magazine* arrived with an offer to lead a new serialized column about the New Woman, complete with essays, illustrations, and practical fashion pieces, many drawn from her own articles and experiences. They wanted her voice and her perspective. And they wanted her in London.

It was the opportunity of a lifetime. Especially after the fiasco of revealing there'd never been a Mr. Capp. She thought for sure her career as a lady correspondent was over.

Still, even as she stirred the soup, she felt the ache of parting. The quiet loss of something she'd once longed for. The laughter with new friends like Lena. The challenging meetings with the Denwall executives. The heady rush of seeing her vision become print.

And Bert.

She could still feel the weight of his gaze that afternoon in the café. The protective brush of his hand on her shoulder. His voice—steady, calm, grounding—when he silenced the gossips with a few simple words.

The gesture had meant something. Maybe not what she'd hoped. But something.

She knew now that he'd forgiven her. Max had stopped by her office and told her so. She only wished Bert had delivered the message himself.

But forgiveness didn't mean a return to the romance, or even friendship, that had budded in the weeks before the ill-fated letter to Ivy.

So, she decided to let it go. Let *him* go.

She'd held her chin high. Focused on the work. Didn't reach for more.

She lifted the spoon to her lips and tasted the slightly too salty soup. Still, she couldn't stop the whisper inside her heart.

I wish he were here.

The knock on her door startled her, and her spoon clattered on the side of the pot.

She wasn't expecting anyone, and the desk porter usually sent word if a visitor was coming.

Wiping her hands on a towel, she crossed the apartment and opened the door.

And froze.

Quentin Ashford, Florence's wayward son, stood there, perfectly composed in his black overcoat, collar dusted with the faintest touch of evening frost.

"Mrs. Capp," he said. "May I come in for a moment?"

Zella stepped aside slowly. "Of course."

He didn't remove his gloves, and she didn't offer him tea. He didn't look like he meant to stay long.

"I wanted to speak with you in person," he said, tone clipped. "I thought you should know ... my mother passed away. Last week."

The words were like a punch to the chest.

Zella caught the edge of a chair to steady herself. "No— no, I hadn't heard. I—I thought she might be traveling. I wrote to her. Twice."

"She died quietly," he said. "In her sleep, at home in Chicago."

Zella pressed a hand to her mouth. "I should have gone to see her. I meant to. I've just been so—"

"I know." Quentin looked away briefly. "She always said you were terribly busy."

Zella tried to speak, but no words came. *Florence. Gone.*

It didn't seem real.

After a long silence, Quentin asked, "Did she write to you recently? In the last few weeks?"

"No. Not since January, I think. Why?"

He hesitated. "She said she wanted to send you something. A letter, maybe. She mentioned it to me in passing."

There was something in his expression that bothered her, but she didn't press him.

He reached into his coat and pulled out a small velvet box.

"She left a few things for you. Personal items. Keepsakes. She said you admired these once."

Zella took the box from his outstretched hand, her fingers suddenly cold.

When she opened it, her breath caught.

A delicate gold bracelet. A brooch in the shape of a lily. And a platinum ring with a deep blue stone. Florence had worn that ring every time they traveled. It had become her signature piece.

"She wanted you to have them," Quentin said.

Zella blinked, and she could feel a tear trail down her cheek. "Thank you. I didn't expect her to leave me anything." She hadn't expected Florence to *leave*.

"Yes, well. She thought highly of you," he said.

There was a pause, and he glanced around her apartment like he was looking for something, but then he stepped back toward the door.

"I won't take any more of your evening," he said. "I thought you should hear the sad news from me directly."

"I'm glad you came," she said quietly.

He nodded briefly and left.

Zella stood in the silence of her apartment, the velvet box in her hands. In the few times she'd seen Quentin when she was Florence's hired companion, he'd always made her feel uncomfortable. He seemed shifty, for lack of a better word.

Yet he was Florence's only child, and Zella didn't like to think badly of anything Florence did. But she'd spoiled Quentin. Once, on a train from Paris to Munich, she'd admitted that she overindulged him after her husband passed away, and worried he'd never be an upstanding man like his father was.

Zella was grateful Quentin lived in Chicago and she'd never see him again, even if he did take the time to bring her the jewelry.

Strange, that. He could've had it sent through Florence's attorney.

She walked slowly to her desk, set the jewelry down, then sank into the chair.

The ring caught the lamplight and gleamed against the dark lining. Zella pressed her fingers to her lips. "I should've gone," she whispered. "I should've made time."

Tears slipped down her cheeks, hot and sudden. She didn't bother brushing them away. If only she'd written more. Visited more. Told Florence what her friendship had meant. Now it was too late.

But the jewelry, a thoughtful gesture, was something. A final word from a woman who had believed in her. Trusted her.

Zella closed the box carefully and held it against her heart. "I'll miss you so," she whispered.

She slowly stood to return to the soup, feeling tired and ancient. She paused, eyes lingering on the dark windowpane where her reflection shimmered. Without Florence, and without Bert, she felt untethered.

"I wish we could have..." she said aloud, her voice cracking.

Could have what?

Even now, it wasn't success or recognition she craved, but Bert's quiet approval. His teasing smile. Him. To share life's joys and heartbreaks.

Zella sank to the floor in the middle of her apartment and allowed herself to grieve. Not just for Florence, but for the loss of something wonderful that would never be.

Still groggy from sleep, she descended the stairs from her apartment. She'd barely managed to eat after Quentin left the night before, and even her usual cup of strong black coffee hadn't cleared the fog.

The desk porter, who'd worked at the Gladstone since its opening, stood when she stepped out of the elevator.

"Mrs. Capp?" he asked in a low voice. "Are you feeling all right this morning?"

Zella tucked a wayward strand of hair behind her ear. She hadn't done the best job of getting dressed this morning, apparently. "I'm fine, thank you. Just didn't sleep very well."

He studied her for a few seconds, and then, as if coming to a decision, inclined his head. He glanced around and motioned her toward the marble column beside the stairwell, away from the morning foot traffic.

"I shouldn't say anything," he muttered, "but you've always been polite to me, and this doesn't sit right."

Her heart began to beat faster. "What doesn't?"

"First, I want to apologize. I shouldn't have let that visitor go up to your apartment last night without letting you know first. He seemed like a nice gent. Well-dressed. Said he was your cousin and wanted to surprise you."

It would've been nice to be warned, but it didn't change anything. She would have permitted Quentin to come up.

"Don't worry. I'm not upset."

"You're such a nice tenant, I didn't think you'd report me or anything. But there's more." He shifted from one foot to the other.

"Yes?"

"He came back to the building about thirty minutes after he left your apartment. Slipped me a folded bill and said a letter or package might be coming for you from Chicago in the next few days. Told me to intercept it. Hand it over to him first."

Zella's stomach dropped. "What did you do?"

He looked away. "At the time, it seemed harmless. He said it was a surprise he wanted to deliver in person. So I took the money and promised I'd watch for the package. But considering how pale you look this morning, I don't think the man is harmless."

Zella nodded slowly. "Thank you for telling me."

He touched the brim of his cap. "If a letter comes, you'll get it first. I swear."

She didn't wait for him to say more. She was already halfway out the door, gloves only half-pulled on, breath catching in her chest. What had Quentin been expecting her to receive? Whatever it was, he didn't want her to know about it.

Florence had always said Quentin was restless. "A beautiful disappointment," she once called him, half laughing. "The kind of son who has the look of an angel while he waits for you to die so he can collect the silver."

But wait. Zella didn't know where to find him. She turned back to the porter. "If Mr. Ashford wanted you to notify him if a letter showed up, he must have planned to stay in the city for a few days. Did he tell you where he was staying?"

"Why, yes, he did. The Ridgeway House at the bottom of Market Street."

Zella hailed a hansom. Something told her she couldn't let this wait.

A few miles and a world away from the Gladstone, the red-bricked lobby of Ridgeway House smelled like cigars and dried flowers—not exactly the sort of place Zella expected Quentin to stay. With the inheritance he'd received from Florence, he could afford to stay anywhere in town. Unless the will hadn't gone through probate yet, which was entirely possible.

She stopped at the front desk and pulled the same trick Quentin used on the Gladstone porter.

"Hello. I'm Frances Ashford. My cousin Quentin is here, and I need to see him immediately. Please tell me his room number." Zella lifted her nose in an imperious air and tapped the scratched oak desk with her gloved forefinger.

"Room 306," the young man sputtered.

Zella took the elevator to the third floor, found 306, and rapped on the door. When it opened, Quentin's eyes widened, then he grimaced.

"Mrs. Capp," he said, voice tight. "I didn't expect a follow-up visit."

"This isn't a social call," she said. "I came to ask why you're paying people off to intercept my mail."

His smile was slow and brittle. "You shouldn't believe everything you hear."

"You shouldn't lie to someone who knows better," she snapped. "Florence sent me a letter before she died, didn't she? And you were hoping it wouldn't reach me."

His hand dropped from the doorknob. "You don't want to do this."

"I'm already doing it."

He stepped back. "Then come in."

Zella hesitated, then followed him inside. The room was stifling. The curtains drawn, a half-empty whiskey glass on the nightstand. A letter opener lay beside it, the blade glinting in a shaft of light.

Quentin pivoted toward her, a strange energy about him now. Not drunk. Not entirely sober. Jittery. Frenzied.

"She was going to give it all to you," he said suddenly. "*You.* And that idiotic charity she clung to like a moral compass."

Zella stiffened. "That can't be true."

"Oh, it is," he snapped. "She wrote it all out in a letter to you that I didn't find out about until right before she passed. She always adored you more than me. Her own son."

Zella shook her head. "Florence was kind. Generous. She doted on you for years. Too much."

Quentin laughed—a short, wild sound. "Well, she cut me out of the will. I saw it before she sent it to her solicitor. In the end, she was too weak to go anywhere, and I saw an opportunity to fix the wrong. Got a new will. Paid a man who knew his ink and his Latin. Looks just like her writing, right down to the loop in the *F*. She left me everything. Just like she should have."

Zella's blood went cold. "You forged a will?"

"I can't let you leave here," he said in a low voice.

Zella took a step back. "You're not serious."

He stared at the letter opener. "I don't have the stomach for murder. But I know men who do. Who owe me favors."

She backed toward the door, trying not to let her panic show. "Quentin, this is insane. You're frightened. You're grieving. But killing me isn't going to fix anything. You'll never get away with it."

"You don't understand," he whispered. "They'll come for me if I don't pay."

He must have some nasty creditors on his back that he'd kill to pay them off.

Zella gripped the doorknob behind her. "Let me go, Quentin. Let me walk out and forget this conversation ever happened. You can have my portion of the will. I'll sign it over to you. Just let me go."

He stared at her for a long moment, then slowly shook his head. "I can't."

TWENTY-FOUR

Bert glanced at the clock in the hall outside his office. Quarter after two. An hour ago, Zella had missed a meeting with the executives to update them on the *Styles Book*.

That alone wasn't cause for panic. She was juggling a dozen final details before the print run. Things slipped. People were late.

But she also hadn't replied to his note. He'd asked her to come to lunch at his parents' house, where he hoped to have a private conversation without it being inappropriate. Even if she didn't want to meet, Zella wasn't the type of petty person to ignore him altogether. She would have delivered her *no* in person, with a witty remark dangling from its end.

He walked to her office, but she wasn't there. He strode to Miss Leighton's desk.

"Do you know where Miss Abbott is?"

"No, I'm sorry, Mr. Walraven. I haven't seen her all morning. I assumed she was at the printer."

She wasn't. He'd sent a messenger there earlier and received a reply that she wasn't expected until tomorrow morning.

He returned to her office and, although he felt bad about it, flipped through her desk calendar. The only thing scheduled for that afternoon was the meeting she had missed. He opened drawers in her desk and rifled through her papers.

Tucked in the back of the bottom drawer, he found two notes.

Mean-spirited, nasty notes. Almost threatening in tone.

His stomach roiled.

Why hadn't she told him she'd received them? At the very least, if she didn't want to talk to him, she could have told Max or James.

He stuck the notes in his pocket and took the elevator to the third floor, heading straight for Max's office.

"Take a look at these," he said, laying them on his friend's desk.

Max leaned back in his chair, eyes scanning each cruel missive. He let out a low whistle. "Are these why Zella wasn't at the meeting today?"

"I don't know why she wasn't there. I can't find her. I was hoping you might know."

Max's eyes widened. "I don't know where she is." He stared at the paper in his hand. "Any idea who might have sent these?"

"No. But I think it must be someone close to her in the office. Someone who could slip in and out without anyone thinking twice about it."

"Like Miss Leighton."

"Exactly. What do we know about her?"

"I think my secretary is friends with her," Max said.

They called the secretary into Max's office, and Bert peppered her with questions. By the time she left, they'd determined that Miss Leighton had been engaged to Howard Turner, a former Denwall employee who, apparently, thought he should be head of the publications department.

"We'll get Miss Leighton up here," Max said.

Ten minutes later, Miss Leighton sat in the chair across from Max's desk while Bert paced the office.

"You're not in trouble," Bert said, "but we need to clear something up."

Miss Leighton's eyes darted from Bert to Max and back. "All right."

Bert kept his voice measured. "Since Miss Abbott's arrival at Denwall, she's experienced several incidents that have caused her to doubt herself, including missed appointments and misplaced documents. Then, private information about her background became public. Frankly, the only way that could have happened was if someone went into her reticule and read her personal mail. As I see it, you're the most likely suspect. You have more access to her office than anyone else at Denwall besides Miss Abbott herself."

Her face twitched. "I—I don't know how those things happened."

Bert stood next to Max's chair so he could look her in the eyes and crossed his arms. "Now, Miss Leighton, we cannot seem to locate Miss Abbott. You didn't send her off on some wild goose chase, did you? Maybe to an appointment she didn't actually have?"

There was a beat of silence, and Miss Leighton's face crumpled.

"I didn't mean for it to go this far," she whispered. "I just wanted her to leave Denwall."

Bert's stomach twisted. Had this woman done something to physically harm Zella? "Where is she? Where's Miss Abbott? If you've hurt her …"

"I don't know where she is. Honestly, I don't. I only moved a few documents. Changed an appointment time on her calendar."

"And sent her threatening notes?"

She hung her head. "Yes."

"Why?" Bert couldn't wrap his mind around wanting to hurt Zella like that.

Her hands twisted in her lap. "Because—because my fiancé was supposed to get the managing director's job. And when he didn't, he left. Said he couldn't stay in Philadelphia while someone less qualified got the position."

She rushed on. "I thought if Miss Abbott was removed, the job might open again, and he might come back. I thought maybe we could get married. I didn't mean to hurt her. I really didn't."

Max narrowed his eyes. "Howard Turner?"

She nodded.

Bert ran a hand down his face. "Miss Leighton, we never seriously considered him. He was quietly under investigation for irregularities in his expense reports. He left because he was caught."

Miss Leighton stared at him as if she didn't understand the words.

"No," she whispered. "He told me it was Denwall politics. That you chose her because she was soon to be a relative. He—"

Bert folded his arms again. "He lied."

She stared at her lap, tears pooling fast. "I'm so sorry. I was stupid. I thought I was protecting something. But he—he used me."

"Yes. He did."

Miss Leighton buried her face in her hands. "I'll resign. I'll turn everything over and pack my desk."

"We'll worry about that later. You're sure you don't know where Miss Abbott is?"

"I'm sure," she whispered. "I have no idea where she went."

After Miss Leighton left Max's office, Max turned to Bert.

"I believe what she's saying, and I don't think she was working with anyone else. So, at least we know there's nothing sinister going on. If Miss Leighton wrote the notes, then there isn't someone else out there who's a threat to Zella." He stood and placed a hand on Bert's shoulder. "Don't worry, she'll show up."

Bert prayed that was the case, but something told him he needed to find Zella—and fast.

Under a partly cloudy sky outside the Denwall building, Bert lifted his collar against the cold even though it was the first day of spring. The wind had started to pick up and everyone in Philadelphia wanted to take a cab rather than walk, it would seem.

Finally, a carriage nosed its way over. When they reached Pine and Eleventh, the carriage stopped outside the Gladstone Apartments. Bert alighted and asked the driver to wait for him, in case he needed the carriage again.

He stepped into the Gladstone lobby and removed his gloves, scanning the quiet space. The desk porter looked up from his register.

"Good afternoon, sir," the man greeted.

"I'm Robert Walraven of Denwall Department Stores. I'm looking for Mrs. Zella Capp." Had she told the Gladstone to refer to her as Miss Abbott yet? "Have you seen her today?"

The porter hesitated. "She's not in, Mr. Walraven. Left earlier today. A bit pale looking, if I do say so."

"Did she say where she was going?"

"No, sir. But I might've upset her, I think. I told her something this morning. About a gentleman who visited her last night."

"What gentleman?"

Zella may be unconventional, but she didn't invite men up to her apartment.

"Tall fellow. Brown hair, slicked back. Expensive coat. He stopped by twice and said he was her cousin. The second time, he offered me money to keep an eye out for a letter from Chicago. Wanted me to give it to him before she saw it."

"Did she know him?"

"I think so. Though she seemed mad that he tried to intercept her mail. Called him something—Ash … Ashbourne? I'm not sure."

Ashbourne. Why did that ring a bell? But it wasn't quite right.

Bert rubbed his temples, trying to recall.

"Ashford!" The porter's voice broke through his thoughts. "The name was Ashford."

The name caught in Bert's mind like a fishhook. He'd heard it before. Months ago, at Will and Ivy's engagement dinner. When Grandmother Shaw quizzed Zella about her life, Zella had mentioned being a traveling companion to a widow named Ashford. Frieda? Frances? No, that wasn't right.

Florence Ashford. That was it. She lived in Chicago, and Bert had the feeling she was too old to travel now. Zella had mentioned in passing that she'd been the woman's traveling companion, yet she'd said it with a softness in her voice that hinted at a cherished friendship. Now this man with the Ashford surname was paying porters for intercepted mail?

"Any chance you know where he's staying?" Bert asked.

The porter bobbed his head. "The Ridgeway House. He mentioned it last night. That's where he wanted me to contact him if a letter from Chicago showed up for Mrs. Capp."

"Thank you," he said as he strode to the front door. Outside, the cab waited as directed. The wind knifed through

Bert's coat and stung his cheeks, but he barely noticed. "The Ridgeway House, please," he said to the driver. "And there's an extra two dollars in it if you can get me there in ten minutes.

The driver tipped his cap. "Yes sir!"

As the cab lurched into motion, Bert leaned forward, elbows on his knees, heart thudding harder with each block they passed.

Was this man Florence Ashford's son? It seemed likely. And what did he want with Zella?

And why did Zella go to him alone?

Maybe she hadn't planned anything, but just reacted. That was what scared him most. Zella, usually so composed, so clever, had looked fragile these past few weeks. Tired. Pulled thin. Bert could have smacked himself for being such a fool, waiting for Zella to come to him. He should have been the one to bridge the gap that had formed between them. Begged her forgiveness for being a prideful, stubborn horse's rump.

And, his heart argued, he should've told her how he felt about her. That he loved her.

If he had, maybe she would have come to him first, before going after Ashford on her own. But he was only just now beginning to admit his feelings to himself.

Bert would beat the man to a pulp if he laid a hand on her.

You might not be able to fix this with your fists. Keep your head.

He closed his eyes and drew a breath that barely reached his lungs.

Lord, I don't know what I'm walking into. But You do. If she's in trouble, guide my steps.

If I'm wrong, stop me.

But if I'm right, please don't let me be too late.

He let the prayer settle in his chest like an anchor, steadier than rage.

As the cab turned toward Ridgeway House, he tensed. He didn't know what Ashford wanted from Zella. But he'd find out soon enough.

TWENTY-FIVE

The world returned slowly—through pain, confusion, and the sour stench of sweat, whiskey, and fear. Zella stirred, but her limbs rebelled. Her wrists were bound tightly behind her back, the rough twine biting into her skin with every slight movement. Her ankles were similarly tied, and her head throbbed where Quentin's open hand had clipped her temple.

A gag pressed into her mouth, the cloth damp with her own breath and knotted cruelly behind her head. When she tried to cry out, the sound lodged behind her teeth, muffled and pitiful.

The empty room was dim, lit only by the flicker of a gaslight behind drawn velvet curtains. She was tied to a hard, high-backed chair shoved in a corner like a discarded piece of furniture.

She'd fought. Oh, she'd fought.

When Quentin turned on her, she tried to flee, but even in his half-drunken stupor, he moved with the rage of a man losing control. He seized her arm and railed against her, saying that she didn't deserve the inheritance Florence had entrusted her with. When she told him his mother was probably worried he'd gamble everything away in the first month, his flat palm came fast. Stars exploded behind her eyes. Then nothing.

She'd regained consciousness with her limbs restrained and a gag in her mouth.

At first, she'd hoped Quentin's decision to hold her was one he'd reconsider. That he'd soon come to his senses. She'd try to talk herself out of the situation if she could, but the gag made it impossible.

He returned, and she realized he wasn't going to change his mind.

Clutching a fresh whiskey bottle, he paced the room, muttering like a man undone. Her hope cracked.

"Just the letter," he growled. "That's all I needed."

Then his voice came quieter and more chilling, "Now she has to die. But not by my hand."

A tremor seized Zella's frame as she strained against the ropes until her skin burned. She shifted slightly to scan for something close by that she could use to help her escape. Her chair scraped against the floor.

"Stop it!" Quentin yelled as he whirled around.

She froze.

He took a swig from the bottle and resumed his pacing. "Where is he?"

Had he hired someone to finish what he couldn't? Panic surged, and her breath came in gasps. She squeezed her eyes shut. *Think. Stay calm.*

But she had nothing. No leverage. No strength. No voice.

But she still had prayer.

Lord of great mercy and salvation, my only hope is in You. You remain faithful, even when I falter. Even when I don't deserve Your love. You see where I am. You know I cannot get out on my own. You are the only one who can save me. I can do nothing but wait on You. I pray this won't be the end of my story on Earth, but if it is, I rest in knowing this won't be my last moment with You. Amen.

A sob caught behind the gag. Her body trembled with each shallow breath. She forced herself to breathe slowly, deliberately. One breath. Then another.

But her thoughts spun, untethered and relentless. *If I die here...*

She'd never again see Central Park in spring. Or be a great-aunt to Ivy's future children. She'd never finish the last pages of the *Styles Book*. She'd never have the chance to tell Bert she loved him.

Bert.

For a brief few days, after they'd kissed at the Academy, she imagined a life with him. Maybe a house in the city with a quiet, book-lined study with a comfortable armchair for him and a writing desk for her. Maybe a Saint Bernard like Ivy's Dickens, lying near the hearth. Laughter and teasing. Cuddling by a well-lit fireplace. Not a fairy tale—a partnership.

But their relationship had imploded, and Bert had lost all respect for her.

Her mind wandered to the offer for a fresh start from *Pall Mall* that sat folded in her drawer. She hadn't committed to it yet—but now?

If I survive, I'll take the position. Not for me. For them. For the Walravens and the Dennisons, who'd been nothing but kind. It would be best for their reputations if they weren't tangled with hers.

And Bert ... he deserves better.

Maybe her final contribution to Denwall wasn't the magazine, after all.

Maybe it was her absence.

A fresh tear escaped.

Quentin's voice pulled her back to the present.

"Where is he?" he growled. "If he doesn't come soon, I'm going to have to take care of this myself."

Zella's eyes flicked toward the entry, praying with every beat of her aching heart that whoever *he* was, he would never make it upstairs. She figured her chances were better against a drunk Quentin than a man who killed for hire.

———

The Ridgeway House lobby was warm and tidy, if a little frayed around the edges. Bert strode to the front desk, where a tired-looking clerk eyed him with raised brows.

"Are you in the right place? This isn't the Bellevue."

Bert offered his most disarming smile, though his pulse roared in his ears and every nerve urged him to shake the man until he gave him what he wanted.

"I'm here to visit Mr. Ashford. He forgot to give me his room number." When the clerk didn't respond, Bert added, "I'm his cousin."

"He's in 306." The clerk eyed him. "Say, is there a family reunion going on up there? You're the second cousin today."

Bert leaned casually against the desk, feigning ease. "Is that so? Female side of the family?"

"That's right. A pretty dark-haired woman. Although you don't look at all alike. She's still up there, as far as I know."

Bert's heart slammed beneath his coat.

"Thanks. I'll join them." He didn't wait for permission, just turned and walked briskly toward the elevator. His hand hovered for half a second ringing the bell for the operator. Too slow and he might lose her. Too fast and he'd tip his hand.

He exited the elevator, glanced down one end of the hallway, then the other—and froze.

A figure, all in dark clothing, was slipping through a fire

escape window just ahead. Bert's stomach tightened. He slowed his stride and followed the man at a steady pace as the stranger crept toward Room 306. Just as he raised a hand to knock, Bert seized him from behind and yanked him away from the door.

"Going somewhere?" he growled.

Startled, the man twisted, but didn't fight. Up close, he appeared younger than expected. Nervous. Sweaty. His desperate expression like that of a starving dog.

"Hey—what's the big idea?" the man hissed.

"I could ask you the same." Bert gave him a firm shake.

The man's eyes darted toward the door.

"Did Ashford send for you?" Bert pressed, lowering his voice.

The man gave a short nod.

"What did he want you for?"

"Wanted me to get rid of some woman for him."

A wave of rage surged through Bert's chest, so sharp and sudden it almost knocked the breath out of him. But anger wouldn't help Zella now. She needed him calm. Focused. Smart.

"I've already alerted the police that a woman's being held here against her will," Bert lied smoothly. "You've got two choices. Tell me what name Ashford knows you by and walk away. Or wait here and explain to the authorities why you came in through a window."

The man scowled. "Jones. Now let me go. I'm not paid enough for this."

Bert didn't release him until both feet were planted firmly on the fire escape. Jones scrambled down the iron ladder like a guilty spider, vanishing into the alley below.

Bert turned toward the door, heart pounding. *Lord, help me. Give me the words. Give me the strength. Please, let her be all right.*

He knocked, and shuffling sounds came from the other side of the door.

The knob rattled and a sallow face peeked through the crack in the doorway. Suspicion flickered across the features that might have been handsome if his eyes weren't bloodshot and his nose not lined with the veins of a heavy drinker.

"Who are you?"

"Jones sent me," Bert said in a low, rough voice. "Something came up. I'm here to take care of your little problem."

Ashford didn't look convinced, but after a beat, he opened the door.

Zella was there. Bound to a chair, gagged, her head drooping forward. But when she lifted her head and their eyes met, a flicker of relief crossed her face. And something else raw and unguarded.

He kept his voice cold, eyes on Ashford. "Untie her. Can't walk a woman through a hotel lobby tied up without raising eyebrows."

He turned a glare on Zella. "And you—wench—you'd best keep quiet."

She nodded, eyes wide but steady.

Ashford grunted and kneeled to untie her feet. Then Bert caught her elbow in a rough, unkind grip. It made his skin crawl to handle her that way, but if Ashford sensed anything was off, they'd never make it out the door.

They reached the threshold before Ashford's voice sliced the air.

"Wait. Something's not right here. That's an expensive coat you're wearing to be acquainted with Jones." In a blink of an eye, he lunged.

But Bert was ready. This wasn't a park bench in Manhattan. He wasn't caught from behind. He shoved Zella to the side, and pivoted, driving one solid punch into Ashford's jaw. The man crumpled with a grunt, hitting the rug in a heap.

Silence reigned, except for Bert's heavy breathing.

He turned to Zella. Her hair had fallen from its pins, and she was shaking. He stepped forward, gently lifted her chin, and brushed her hair back from her face to reveal an ugly bruise.

"You're safe now," he said, voice soft.

Her eyes filled. He untied the gag first, then her wrists, his fingers trembling more than he liked. The ropes had bitten into her skin. He stared at the angry red lines for a moment before moving to the man on the floor.

Using the same ropes, Bert bound Ashford's hands tightly behind his back and stuffed the gag in his mouth for good measure.

When he was finished, Zella stood and flung her arms around him, burying her face in his coat.

"Thank you, Bert ... for rescuing me." Wool muffled her voice. "How did you find me?"

"I asked the right questions, I guess." He looked down at her wrists again, then met her eyes. "I should've gotten here sooner."

"No," she whispered. "You came exactly when I needed you."

He helped her straighten and took her hand. "Let's get you out of here. I'll tell the front desk to alert the police, and after that I'm taking you to my parents." He pointed a finger when she opened her mouth. "No argument. I'm not leaving you alone. If the police want us for questioning, they can find us at Rittenhouse Square."

"I'm not arguing. I don't want to be alone." She slipped her arm through his and leaned into him as they walked into the hallway. They didn't speak for a few steps.

"Wait," she said and peered up at him, her eyes twinkling despite everything she'd endured. "Did you call me a *wench* back there?"

"It was the only tough-guy word I could come up with in the moment." He shrugged, mouth twitching.

She let out a hoarse laugh. "Remind me to buy you an eye patch."

⁂

Zella winced at the pain in her wrists as she shifted on the Walravens' brocade settee. Sunlight filtered through the curtains, and a clock ticked steadily on the mantel.

Several hours had passed since Bert had rescued her from Quentin's hotel room, and she'd been fussed over by Bert and his family for most of that time. She still wore her wrinkled walking dress, but now a blanket lay tucked around her legs, and a pillow cushioned her head. Someone—the Walraven butler, perhaps—had brought her tea, but it had gone cold.

Two police inspectors stood near the fireplace. One was older, grizzled, with gray whiskers and a skeptical frown. The other, younger and with a kinder demeanor, flipped through a notepad. Scowling fiercely, Bert stood beside the settee with his arms crossed tightly.

He put guard dogs to shame.

"Miss Abbott," the older officer began, "you confirm that you went to Quentin Ashford's hotel of your own volition, but then he forcibly detained you?" Although factually correct, the officer's tone bordered on accusatory.

Bert dropped his arms and stepped toward the man. "Now look here. Miss Abbott is a guest in our home."

"Bert, it's all right," Zella said quickly, before the scene ended with him in handcuffs for slugging an officer of the law. "The officer has a valid question."

She turned her eyes from Bert's ticking jaw to the officer. "I know Quentin Ashford well. I'm good friends with his mother. After he came to my apartment to inform me of her death, he made a point to tell the Gladstone Apartment porter to detain my mail."

When the officer only harrumphed, it was her turn to fold her arms. "I may have reacted too quickly in my anger over Quentin's high-handedness, but I honestly never imagined him to be a danger to me." Her voice wavered a bit on those last words. Oh, she hated sounding weak.

Bert laid a hand on Zella's shoulder, as if to bolster her courage.

"But when I arrived at the hotel," she continued, "he pulled me into the room and bound and gagged me." Her words came out hoarse, but at least they were now steady. "At some point, he admitted he'd hired someone to kill me."

The older officer's brows shot up. "Why would he want to kill you?"

"Because his mother left me half of her fortune, and I got the feeling he received very little. Certainly not enough to cover his gambling debts."

The officer made a note. "And this man, Jones. The one Mr. Walraven encountered on the fire escape. Do you know him?"

"Only what Mr. Walraven told me. Quentin referred to someone who would 'take care of the problem' for him, but he didn't name names."

The younger inspector cleared his throat. "We believe the man Mr. Walraven saw was Dickie Jones. He's a known associate of minor criminal rings around the docks. We've got patrols out across the neighborhood. If he's smart, he'll surrender. And if he does, he'll likely testify against Ashford. Jones will want to cut a deal."

Zella gripped the armrest of the settee. "So you believe me?"

The older officer looked up, surprised. "Miss, with your

injuries, the witness statement from Mr. Walraven, and a gagged man tied up on the floor of a Ridgeway House hotel room? Yes, we believe you. But it is our duty to ask questions, even ones that may be uncomfortable for the victim."

"Most likely," the younger officer interjected, "the prosecutors will charge Ashford with multiple counts, including kidnapping, unlawful imprisonment, attempted fraud, and depending on what Jones confirms, conspiracy to commit murder. He's not going anywhere for a long time."

Zella nodded slowly. A strange quiet settled inside her. Not peace, exactly. Relief warred with sadness—sadness for Florence that her son would turn out to be such a wastrel. Not everything can be blamed on one's parents. Some people were just rotten.

The officers left with polite nods and a promise to follow up. The butler showed them out, and the parlor door clicked shut behind them. Silence settled in the room, as only Zella and Bert remained.

She exhaled. Only then did she realize she'd been holding her breath.

Bert moved to her side without a word and sat on the edge of the armchair next to her. He didn't reach for her. Didn't try to fill the silence.

"Thank you," she said quietly. "For everything. For finding me. For being calm when I couldn't be."

"I wasn't calm. I just pretended well."

"Then you're a better actor than I gave you credit for."

He leaned closer and grasped her hand. "Out in that hotel hallway, when the full realization of what was happening hit me, I was scared to death I'd never see you again. Never have the opportunity to tell you how sorry I am. To make it right."

"What are you sorry for?" Her heart pitter-pattered as he rubbed his thumb in soft circles on her palm.

"For being so distant after the truth of your marriage came

out. I thought I was protecting myself. Really, I was punishing you for something that wasn't your fault. I let the insidious feeling of pride and inflated self-worth convince me you didn't tell me sooner because you didn't respect our relationship enough. That was selfish of me. I'm sorry."

She met his gaze, her throat tightening, but she nodded. Those lovely eyes that his wire-rimmed spectacles couldn't hide were full of compassion. And something else she didn't dare let herself hope for.

TWENTY-SIX

The grounds of Fairmount Park bustled with color and motion. Bert smiled as dozens of children from the Franklin Street Orphanage darted through the grass, searching for painted eggs tucked among tree roots and shrubs.

Like every Easter for the past five years, the Denwall Annual Egg Hunt had drawn a cheerful crowd. He'd heard that the Walnut Street parade had been rather subdued this year, with fewer spectators lining the streets after services. Too chilly, perhaps, for Philadelphia's high society willing to make a fashionable spectacle of themselves.

But here, in the open sprawl of the park, joy bloomed freely. No one seemed to mind the brisk air that tugged at coat hems and brought color to cheeks. Laughter rang through the budding trees.

Tulips and daffodils painted the flowerbeds in soft pastels, while kites soared above the lawns in dips and swirls. White bunting fluttered between benches, and a string quartet played a lilting waltz beneath a striped tent that billowed gently in the breeze.

Bert stood near a shallow creek that wound through the

west side of the park, and he helped a gang of rowdy boys fold paper boats. One of the vessels capsized almost immediately, to the dismayed howls of its young captain. Bert chuckled with the group but found his gaze drifting again and again to Zella.

If he let his mind wander to what could have happened to her at the hands of Ashford and Jones, his stomach roiled like an ocean in a storm. When he'd entered the hotel room and seen Zella bound and gagged, it was all he could do not to roar like a wounded lion. He'd never been so scared in his life, not even when he was attacked in Madison Square Park. Now, two weeks after Zella's kidnapping, he still woke up in a cold sweat every night.

Thank you, Lord, for showing me the way to her and for giving me the strength to get her out of the situation alive and unharmed.

He shook his head and forced himself to focus on the good in life. To focus on Zella, who in all honesty took his breath away.

She wore a soft blue dress with cream gloves, her dark hair pinned high and looped with daisy chains courtesy of the smallest girls in attendance. She crouched near the lemonade table, laughing with a child who'd mistaken a pink pebble for a precious gem. Zella's joy was unguarded, genuine. Watching her, something inside Bert loosened—something he hadn't realized was clenched.

"You've found your true calling," he said when he stepped up behind her.

"With children?" She tipped her head, and the look on her face caused his heart to thud.

"With flower crowns. But yes, also children."

Zella glanced at the pack of youngsters now chasing a boy who'd cheated by smuggling a second basket. "I didn't expect to enjoy it," she admitted. "But there's something wonderful about the way they laugh with their whole bodies."

"You looked beautiful at church this morning," Bert said quietly.

Her cheeks flushed. "You clean up well yourself."

Did she realize her loveliness on the inside far surpassed her beauty on the surface? Although she hadn't told him herself, he'd discovered from Myra that she'd donated her entire inheritance from Florence Ashford to the orphanage. Yet, she hadn't said a word to anyone. Myra only knew because James sat on their board of directors.

Her selflessness floored him.

"Would you care to go for a walk?" Bert held out his arm.

She grinned and slipped her arm through his. "I'd be delighted."

They strolled the edges of the lawn, past budding dogwood and carefully placed benches meant more for admiring the view than resting tired feet. When they passed a wide sycamore tree with its mottled trunk thick enough to hide a pair of full-grown adults, Bert gently pulled her behind it.

A breeze stirred the leaves overhead, scattering light across the grass. For a heartbeat, the world stilled. Just the two of them, wrapped in spring and silence.

He slipped his arms around her waist and tugged her closer. She tipped her face to his with a soft smile, and he bent to give her a quick kiss. He'd love to linger longer, but he respected her reputation too much.

When they parted, her breath caught. "What was that for?"

"Because I've wanted to do that since the Charity Ball." He brushed a knuckle along her cheek. "And because you look like spring personified. Thank you for being here."

"I'm glad you invited me."

He'd known from the start that her move to Philadelphia wasn't permanent. The moment Harlan announced that Zella was coming to Philadelphia to lead the *Styles Book*, Bert knew she'd return to New York when the job was finished. Still, he'd allowed himself to hope she'd find a reason to stay, and he prayed it would be her idea. The last thing he wanted was to guilt her into staying.

They stood in silence a moment longer, then returned to the green, where the children shrieked with delight and the Denwall volunteers attempted to herd them into a semi-orderly line for the carriage ride back.

From several feet away, Bert watched Zella as she crouched to help three girls who had gotten more raspberry jam on their cheeks than in their mouths. When she lifted her head and caught him staring, he gave her a sheepish shrug. She beamed, seemingly unbothered.

After the carriages had rolled away, the remaining volunteers gathered near the refreshment tent, where Myra handed out the last of the teacakes.

"I had no idea egg hunts could be this exhausting," Zella said, accepting a glass of lemonade.

"They are," Myra replied, brushing crumbs from her hands. "But it's the good kind of tired." She gave them both a knowing grin before disappearing into a circle of chattering women.

Zella and Bert each took one of the final cakes and wandered to a nearby bench, where they sat in companionable silence, the spring sun warming their shoulders.

"You have sugar on your cheek," Zella teased, reaching out to brush the corner of his mouth with a fingertip. Their eyes met, and Bert wished they were behind the sycamore again.

He cleared his throat. "So, when the *Styles Book* is done, what will you miss most?"

"Not the deadlines or the budget discussions," she said with a grin. "But ... maybe the sense of doing something that matters. And the camaraderie. That took time to build."

Bert nodded slowly. "You were generous with Sylvia Leighton. After all she did, you gave her a glowing reference. You didn't have to."

"I understood her motives." Her eyes didn't waver from his face. "Desperation makes people do foolish things. Especially when they're losing someone they love."

Bert looked down, the words sinking deep. He had a feeling he'd understand that kind of ache all too soon. Of losing someone you loved. And he loved Zella Abbott with his entire being.

"I wish we could stay in this day a little longer," he murmured.

Zella didn't speak right away. When she did, her voice was steady. "Then let's promise to remember it."

His eyes met hers. "Deal."

⊹─────⊹

Zella's heart ached.

She sat with Bert on the park bench, a teacake next to her, untouched. The remnants of the Easter celebration lingered around them. Ribbons tangled in the grass, the distant clink of lemonade glasses being packed away, the rustle of skirts and jackets as volunteers drifted off in twos and threes. Laughter still echoed faintly, as if the park itself refused to let the day end.

But it would. And so would this season of her life.

She tipped her head toward the pale sky, squinting against the brightness. London would be gray and damp by comparison. Grand in its own way, yes, but so far away.

She glanced sideways at Bert, who sat forward with his elbows on his knees, eyes trained on the emptying park. The lines at the corners of his mouth had deepened these past few months, carved by worry and wear, and softened now by whatever quiet peace this day had brought him.

She didn't want to leave him. Not really.

She'd told herself from the beginning that this arrangement, this city, this role, and then this man were only temporary—a bridge between her past and a promising future of her own making. But now that the bridge was nearly crossed, her steps slowed.

Would telling him she was going to London change anything? Or would it only complicate what remained?

She could picture it too easily—his quiet disappointment, the guarded look returning to his eyes, the polite congratulations masking a thousand things unsaid. No. She wouldn't tell him yet. Not until the *Styles Book* launched. Not until she could say goodbye without falling apart.

A breeze stirred, lifting a curl at her temple. Somewhere behind them, a child's shoe clacked against a stone, followed by a mother's patient murmur. Life kept moving, as it always did.

"Penny for your thoughts?" Bert nudged Zella's shoulder with his.

"They'd cost more than that today."

He chuckled, though something flickered in his gaze. Concern, maybe. Or curiosity. Yet she didn't offer more. Instead, she rose and smoothed her skirt. "Shall we help with cleanup?"

"Lead the way."

They moved toward the refreshment table, picking up stray bits of trash as they went. Not touching again, but close enough that she could smell Bert's bay rum cologne and feel the quiet strength of his presence. The setting sun slanted gold through the trees and painted their shadows long across the grass.

Zella memorized the feel of the path beneath her boots,

the scent of hyacinth curling through the air, the warmth of Bert's nearness.

She would leave. But not yet.

For now, she would walk beside him, hold the ache quietly, and let the day linger just a little longer.

TWENTY-SEVEN

A line formed outside Denwall long before the doors opened.

Bert stood at the second-floor railing overlooking the main floor. Through the window, he could see the crowd gathered on the sidewalk, spilling into the street. The buzz in the air felt more like opening night at the opera than the launch of a fashion book.

For two weeks, newspapers had carried the advertisement Zella had written herself. She'd waxed poetic about the many wonders to be found in the eighty-page *Denwall's European Styles Book*—how, with a minimum purchase, it could be any shopper's for free. Or, if they wanted it outright, they could buy it at a Denwall counter for one dollar.

When the front doors finally swung open, the orderly but eager crowd surged forward. Customers streamed into the store in pairs and clusters, heels clicking on marble, chatter rising like magpies gathering in a tree. Clerks stood ready behind glass counters, where stacks of the *Styles Book* waited.

James appeared beside Bert with an expression of mild astonishment. "I haven't seen a crowd like this since ... well, I'm not sure I ever have."

Bert gave a wordless nod, arms crossed, eyes still trained on the scene below. They had planned for a good day, and he had prayed for a strong response. But this?

Two women flipped through the pages of the book, their gloved fingers pointing with delight. One turned it to show a friend, eyes wide. Another began pulling items off the shelf, matching them to a page like puzzle pieces coming to life. A gentleman in a monocle called over a clerk to ask about a Turkish rug featured in the Home Décor section.

It was happening.

Conversion, Harlan would call it.

Magic, Zella would say with a grin.

"It's working," James murmured, his voice tinged with awe. "They're shopping from the page."

"Exactly what she designed it to do," Bert said quietly.

Zella had created this moment not just with her mind, but with her whole being. Every clever headline, every carefully curated illustration, was a piece of her. And her name appeared just inside the cover, in modest type beneath the masthead. But there it was, for all the world to see. *Zella Abbott*.

And they were talking about her.

"Did you see the illustrations in the women's fashion section? A woman chose them. Not a man."

"It's about time!"

"Did you read her article about pretending to be a widow so she could work as a lady correspondent?"

"Good for her!"

Bert descended the staircase to the main floor. He wanted to spend this moment with Zella and tell her how proud he was of her, but he couldn't find her anywhere.

As he passed by the women's jewelry counter, he overheard a young woman ask brightly, "Do we know when the next issue is coming?"

"There isn't one, I'm afraid," the clerk replied. "It's a one-time, special publication—so hold on to it like an heirloom."

An heirloom. Bert almost smiled.

He passed by a woman and her tired-looking husband.

"Must you read it now? Buy the thing and read it at home," the man grumbled.

She patted his arm, her eyes never leaving the book. "In a minute, dear. This is so fascinating. All about the New Woman."

Her husband rolled his eyes. "Heaven help us."

Bert chuckled as he moved past. Where was she? The last time he'd seen Zella, an hour remained before the store opened.

He took the stairs to the home goods section and found her near the fancy dinnerware. Wearing the same green walking suit she'd worn on her first day, she stood gazing at a display, her finger tapping against her chin.

He approached without announcing himself. "What are you doing hiding back here?"

"I'm not," she said without looking up. "But this fancy dinner display looks off balance."

"Tragedy."

Her lips twitched.

"You did it," he said, wishing they were alone so that he could swing her around in a circle to celebrate the moment.

"*We* did it." She turned back, nudging a dessert plate into alignment with care. "Have you spoken to James?" she asked over her shoulder.

"Briefly. He's beside himself. He thinks we'll have lines for days."

"I'm glad." Zella gave him a tentative smile. "Would you walk with me? Let's go up to the lunchroom, if you don't mind. No one will be there yet."

"Of course." He wouldn't refuse a moment alone with

her, but his heart felt heavy. Whatever she wanted to tell him seemed to dim the light in her eyes.

She led the way to the rear staircase, where polished brass railings curved toward the upper floors. Clerks bustled on the main level below, but with each step, the noise of the crowd faded behind them. They passed a portrait of Father in the stairwell, his stern gaze fixed somewhere above their heads.

The lunchroom was empty and blessedly quiet.

Zella moved to a table, pulled out a chair, and sat. Bert did the same across from her. He rested his forearms on the table-top, hands clasped, and waited for her to say what was weighing on that pretty head of hers.

She cleared her throat. "I've accepted an offer from *Pall Mall Magazine*."

Bert froze. "You ... what?"

"They want me in London by the end of April. They're giving me a daily column. And they're hiring me as Zella Abbott."

The words sank like stones. "They don't care about the name change?"

"They think it adds mystique." She gave a faint laugh. "More importantly, they believe my work speaks for itself. That I've proved I don't need to pretend anymore."

Bert swallowed. "And you're going?"

"I am."

He reached across the table and gently grasped her hand. "You could stay."

"I can't." Her voice was steady. "The job is over. We knew I'd head back to New York once the *Styles Book* launched."

"But you're not heading back to New York. You're going clear across the ocean." He tried to keep the panic from his voice.

"This is a wonderful opportunity. One no one else is offering me right now."

She was right, of course. Her career mattered most, and she needed to go where the best work waited. But it hurt like the dickens. He'd accepted New York. They'd be only a short train ride apart, but that was no longer on the table.

"Will I see you before you go?"

"I won't leave until after Ivy and Will's wedding." She gave him a cheeky grin. "And there's the party at the Dennisons' tonight. I'll save you a dance."

"I wouldn't miss it for the world." Even if it broke his heart.

⊹⊶⊷⊹

The chandelier above the Dennison ballroom glittered with enough light to outshine the stars, casting a golden warmth over the polished floors and the guests in their evening best. Strains of a waltz drifted from the piano, and the fire crackled.

Zella stood near the far window, a glass of punch in her hand, watching the evening unfold with an odd sense of stillness.

It was all happening around her, but not with her—the laughter, the rustle of evening gowns, and the strains of a waltz mingled with tinkling crystal ware. Every few minutes someone new would mention the *Denwall's European Styles Book*, and she'd catch fragments of praise that floated like rose petals in a breeze.

"Inspired ..."

"Brilliantly curated ..."

"My sister's already trying to copy the French parlor arrangement on page sixteen ..."

And her name. Her name was on their lips. Spoken aloud in admiration. In recognition.

She should have felt triumphant. Instead, she felt like she was going to shatter into a thousand pieces.

"Oh, there you are." Myra appeared in a rustle of sapphire taffeta, her cheeks flushed from laughter. "I've been looking everywhere. James wants to toast you soon, and I told him you might run off if we didn't act quickly."

"I'd never run from praise," Zella said with a grin.

"But you might run from sentiment." Myra gave her a fond nudge. "They adore you, darling. You've done something rare. Something real. Come, bask in it."

Before Zella could reply, a familiar voice floated from behind them.

"I'll see she gets there, Myra," Bert said.

She turned to take in the one person she wanted to be with above all others. His tie was slightly askew, his hair just windblown enough to suggest he hadn't lingered long in front of a mirror. But his eyes—steady and unreadable—were fixed on her.

Zella's breath caught.

"I'll meet you at the front of the room then," Myra said, eyes twinkling. With a knowing smile, she drifted back into the crowd.

Zella took a slow sip of her drink, then walked toward him. "You're here."

"Of course," he said simply.

The silence between them stretched, and something in her chest squeezed.

"Miss Abbott," a woman's cultured voice came from Zella's left. She prayed it wasn't another society ambush, like the one at the Palm Café.

Zella turned and pasted a smile on her face.

"I'm Joyce Harrison." The woman extended her hand, and Zella took it in a light handshake. "I just wanted to apologize."

"Apologize? Whatever for?"

Mrs. Harrison looked Zella in the eyes. "I was with Prudence Langley that day at the Palm Café. I'm ashamed that I didn't stop her or stand up for you. What she did was wrong, and I'm sorry for it." She hesitated and her gaze took in the crush of people in the ballroom. "By the looks of things, you don't need my support, but I give it anyway. I applaud what you've done, even if I don't condone deception."

Zella gave the kind woman a small smile. "Nor do I, and I'm not proud of mine, but I hope to move past it." She reached out and touched Mrs. Harrison's forearm. "Thank you. You coming over here means the world."

"You're welcome. Enjoy your party."

Before Zella could reply, Ivy's sweet voice caught her attention.

"Ivy?" Zella said aloud, turning. She handed Bert her glass of punch and squealed in delight. Yes, she, Zella Abbott, the epitome of poise and confidence, squealed. Her arms flew around Ivy's shoulders, and tears flowed freely from her face.

"Surprise!" Ivy said, her eyes bright. "We took the express train."

Zella laughed and pulled Will into a fierce, joyful hug. "Thank you for bringing her," she whispered in his ear.

"Everyone's talking about the magazine in Manhattan," Ivy told her as she looped her arm through Zella's.

"She's not exaggerating," Will said, grinning. "You've caused quite a stir, Zella."

Zella flushed, but her heart swelled. "Thank you. I—" She stopped when the announcer declared the first waltz of the evening.

Will gently pulled Ivy's arm. "I believe you promised me the first dance. Plus, it will give me an excuse to put my arms around my beautiful fiancé." Before they moved away, he winked at his brother.

Bert set down the punch glass he'd held since Zella handed it to him, and he searched her face. "May I have this dance?"

Her heart fluttered like a thousand butterflies. "I'd be honored."

After the first two dances, both of which she danced with Bert, Zella found Ivy and they slipped away from the hum of the ballroom and into the dim, quiet parlor down the hall. Ivy perched on the edge of a chaise while Zella paced, then stopped.

"There's something I need to tell you."

Ivy's eyes widened. "What's wrong?"

"Nothing to worry about, pet. I received an offer from *Pall Mall Magazine.* They want me to write a series on the New Woman. Editorials, features, profiles. They've asked me to come to London." Zella had planned to tell Ivy after the wedding, but she'd learned her lesson about keeping secrets.

Ivy's hand flew to her throat, her blue eyes bright with emotion. "Zella, that's incredible."

"You think so?"

"I do. I'm thrilled for you." Ivy reached for her hand and gave it a squeeze. "Even if I'll miss you like mad."

Zella sat beside her, shoulders relaxing for the first time all day. "I wasn't sure how you'd feel."

"I think," Ivy said, "that every woman deserves to walk through the door God opens for her. And if that door is halfway across the world, then so be it."

They both laughed softly, and Zella leaned her head on Ivy's shoulder for a moment, grateful beyond words.

"You'll write and..." Ivy stopped. "You'll be here for the wedding, won't you?"

Zella chuckled. "With bells on."

From the ballroom came a rising cheer—James Dennison calling for the last toast of the night.

Zella stood, smoothing her skirt. "Time to go back."

"Don't wait too long to tell Bert," Ivy said gently. "He deserves to hear it from you."

"I told him earlier." Zella's throat clogged with emotion.

They rejoined the party, stepping once more into the clamor of celebration. And across the room, near the hearth, Bert stood watching her.

Something in her heart told her she'd stay in Philadelphia. If only he'd ask.

Twenty-Eight

Zella paused at the top of the staircase leading down to the church vestibule, one hand resting lightly on the polished rail. Music floated up from below, the warm chords from the old organ, along with the soft rustle of fabric as guests shifted in the pews. For one suspended moment, she let it wash over her. The joy. The hope.

She descended slowly, her bridesmaid's gown whispering against the wooden stairs.

The sanctuary glowed in the late morning light, tall stained-glass windows casting ripples of ruby and sapphire across the aisle. White ribbons adorned the pews, and sprays of cream roses framed the chancel. The organ shifted to a gentler tune as the final guests took their seats.

Zella waited in the narthex with the other bridesmaids, who included a few friends from their cycling club and Caroline Walraven. A few feet away, Bert adjusted his cuffs with deliberate calm, but she noticed the way his jaw ticked and his shoulders held tension beneath the elegant lines of his navy coat.

When he stepped beside her and offered his arm, she hesitated only a moment before taking it.

"You clean up well," she said—a line she'd used with him before, but one that grounded her now as they waited for the signal to proceed.

"You don't look so bad yourself," he replied. The corner of his mouth lifted, but the attempt at levity didn't quite reach his hazel eyes.

The music swelled, and they stepped into the aisle, walking in measured time past rows of smiling guests—the beaming faces of people who loved Ivy and Will.

At the front, Zella caught sight of Jemima seated beside Laura, with Charles on the other side. Jemima's eyes misted the moment she saw her, and Zella gave her a soft, reassuring smile as she passed.

When they reached the altar, Bert gently released her arm. He moved to stand beside Will, while Zella took her place among the bridesmaids. The hush that followed seemed to ring with expectation.

Then the music shifted again, and everyone stood.

Ivy appeared at the back of the church, radiant. Light caught the lace of her veil, the soft sheen of satin, the flush in her cheeks that had nothing to do with the rouge Zella had lightly applied earlier and everything to do with the man waiting at the altar.

Zella's breath snagged in her chest.

Ivy had been beautiful before—in the way she loved books, in her quiet resolve, in the fierce loyalty that ran deep as bedrock. But today, she glowed. She was becoming someone's wife. And not just anyone's. Will Walraven adored her. It was in every glance he gave her. Together, they'd build a lovely future for themselves.

The vows were eloquent and heartfelt. The kiss earned a soft ripple of applause, quickly hushed by the officiant's gentle voice. Then the guests rose again, lining the center aisle as Ivy and Will stepped into it, arm in arm, to walk out together into their new life.

Bert stepped beside Zella once more. "Ready?" he asked, offering his arm again.

She gave a little nod. "Lead the way, Mr. Walraven."

Outside, flower petals caught the breeze, and laughter rang across the steps of the church. As the guests spilled into the street, Zella shifted slightly toward Bert.

"You're quiet," he said.

"I'm thinking."

"Dangerous."

She looked at him. "I was imagining what it would feel like."

"To get married?"

She nodded.

Something flickered in his expression. Hope? Surprise? Regret? It passed quickly, replaced by the composed mask of a man still weighing the contents of his own heart.

"You'd make a formidable wife," he said at last. "God help the poor man who tries to keep up with you."

Zella laughed softly, but her heart clenched.

The wedding party and guests gathered at Ivy and Will's new home for a wedding breakfast and reception. Will's father gave a toast with tears in his eyes. He even praised the choice Will had made in a wife.

How the mighty had fallen.

When the guests had mostly gone, Zella embraced Ivy once again—tighter this time—and Ivy's soft hair pressed against Zella's cheek.

"I won't see you before I leave for London, since you'll be on your honeymoon," Zella whispered. "But I'll write you from the ship."

Ivy pulled back slightly. "With everything going on, I hadn't realized you were leaving so soon."

"A week from yesterday." Should she be more excited? The job was the chance of a lifetime, yet her chest felt hollow. Would she ever again experience what she'd had in her six months in Philadelphia? The highs and the lows. The excitement. Falling in love.

"You'll be brilliant," Ivy said.

"I hope so. And *you'll* have your happily ever after."

"You deserve one too."

Zella smiled. "Maybe someday."

That evening, in her quiet apartment, Zella began packing boxes. The *Pall Mall* job was long term, so there was no reason to keep renting the place.

She opened her desk drawer, pulled out the framed photograph of her make-believe husband, and tossed it in the trash bin.

In a few weeks, she'd be writing full time as Zella Abbott. In London.

Unless something changed.

TWENTY-NINE

Zella stood on the upper deck of the *Majestic*, her gloved fingers wrapped tightly around the ship's railing. Her trunk had already been hoisted aboard, and the steward had shown her to a small room.

The ship loomed like a sleeping beast against the pier, its funnels exhaling lazy puffs of steam into the pale dawn. Fog drifted in from the harbor, curling around the hull like ribbon. Everything felt suspended and unreal.

She wasn't the only passenger at the railing. As tradition demanded, travelers lined the upper decks, waving down to the crowd of well-wishers below. The hum of voices mingled with the calls of gulls and the low churning rhythm of the engines as they warmed.

On the dock, families embraced. Mothers gave last-minute instructions to daughters while they dabbed at their cheeks with gloved fingers. Fathers clapped their sons on the back with smiles that couldn't hide the sting of parting.

Zella's eyes snagged on a woman in a feathered hat who sobbed into a lace-trimmed handkerchief, her husband patting her back with helpless affection. It made something in her chest ache.

Jemima had offered to come and wave her off, but Zella said no. She couldn't bear to see her cry again. Couldn't promise, one more time, that she was fine. That this was what she wanted.

It was. *Wasn't it?*

Dockhands shouted clipped commands, and the bell clanged a second warning. Steam hissed beneath her feet. The ship groaned like it was waking up.

She had promised herself she wouldn't cry. She'd told no one how afraid she was. Leaving no longer felt brave. It just felt hollow.

Her thoughts wandered through Ivy's wedding and the applause that followed the launch of the *Styles Book*, through the daisy crown a little girl had placed on her head during the Easter egg hunt, declaring Zella a princess.

And then, inevitably, she thought of Bert. Quiet, steady Bert. Infuriatingly calm, maddeningly reserved, and yet so present. The way he came after her when she'd been kidnapped, and how he fussed over her at his parents' home afterward. The look in his eyes when he kissed her on the balcony at the Academy of Music. The moment she knew she loved him.

Some ridiculous, foolish part of her had imagined he might be at the ship's departure. That he would come. That he would stop her.

But of course, he hadn't.

A steward passed by and tipped his cap politely. "We're casting off shortly, miss. They're about to lift the gangplanks."

Zella nodded, but didn't move. Her grip on the railing tightened.

"Going somewhere without saying goodbye?"

The voice hit her like a ripple of heat.

She turned.

Bert stood there, overcoat flapping slightly in the breeze. His hair was damp from the mist, and behind his spectacles, his lovely hazel eyes held something unreadable. Hope, maybe. Or fear. Or both.

"I thought we already said goodbye at the wedding reception," she managed.

"I thought so too." He stepped closer, his boots tapping the deck with each stride. "But I have news. Something I thought you should know before you left."

She held her breath.

"The board voted yesterday. Full approval. They want three issues of the *Styles Book* each year."

Zella blinked. "Three?"

"They want you to run it," he said. "Total editorial freedom. Complete authority. You'd have your own department. A full staff."

She couldn't speak.

"They want you to stay," he added gently. "They need you. But more than that—" He paused. "*I* want you to stay. Not just as our managing editor... but as my wife."

Zella's heart soared, but her mind scrambled to keep up. His words felt like paper birds—weightless, beautiful, impossible.

A bell rang again, louder now. Urgent. The final call. Dockhands moved quickly, shouting as the gangway prepared to lift.

She glanced toward the pier, then back to him.

"This was my clean break," she whispered. "A new chapter. A fresh start."

"We'll write new chapters," Bert said, his voice quiet but firm.

Zella exhaled slowly, the weight of everything pressing into her ribs. "My things are already in my stateroom."

"I asked a porter to take them back to the dock." A hint of his crooked smile broke through the bold declaration. "I took a chance."

"You're very sure of yourself."

"I'm sure of you. Of us." When she didn't speak, he hesitated, no longer looking quite so confident. "I love you and I'm sorry it's taken me so long to say that. The offer of marriage is on your terms. Wherever you are, that's where I want to be. So if you'd rather, I'll come with you to London. We don't have to live in Philadelphia."

Her heart soared at the sacrifice he was willing to make for her. "I love Philadelphia. I don't want to go to London." She beamed up at him. "I love you, Robert Walraven, and I'd love to be your wife."

He whooped, grabbed her waist, and spun her around.

When he set her down, they walked back toward the gangway, passing startled passengers who stared in confusion at the couple stepping off instead of on.

One older gentleman chuckled and tipped his hat. "Changed your mind, miss?"

"No." Zella gave him a wink. "I never change my mind. I alter it to accommodate the current environment."

Once on the dock, Bert took her hand, and they walked toward the pierhead. The *Majestic*'s whistle blew, and the gangway clattered as the dockworkers pulled it away from the ship.

Zella didn't look back. Didn't need to. Everything she wanted was beside her.

EPILOGUE

Four months later

The garden behind the Walraven summer home in Bryn Mawr had never looked finer. Laura patted herself on the back for a job well done.

Pale linen bunting fluttered from trellises, and fresh-cut roses burst from every vase, urn, and bowl. A string quartet played beneath the shade of an old sycamore, the soft notes threading through conversations like ribbons.

Bert and his new bride stood under an arch of yellow roses as they chatted with the St. Crispin's pastor who'd officiated their wedding ceremony.

Zella still held her bouquet—a tumble of blush peonies and creamy tea roses—tightly in her grasp. She'd promised to toss it to the unmarried women by the end of the evening.

Behind them, Ivy and Will stood with Caroline as they laughed at something Ned said. Laura now watched her daughter. Tall and beautiful, always a bit wild, always the first to challenge her brothers. Caroline would never settle for less than love.

And Laura wouldn't have it any other way.

Laura's gloved hands folded neatly at her waist. She glanced at Myra, who stood beside her in a powder blue gown and a hat weighed down with feathers that refused to behave in the breeze.

"Would you look at them?" Myra whispered, fanning herself. "They could have stepped out of a romance novel."

Laura grinned at her friend. "Bert never looked so certain of anything."

"And Zella..." Myra sighed. "Radiant, of course. Though I half expected her to wear something more outlandish."

"Jean-Philippe Worth sent her that gown. Said she'd look beautiful in it."

Myra tilted her head. "I suppose the marriage means Denwall has lost her as editor of the *Styles Book*."

"I don't think so. Zella plans to stay on and Bert encouraged her to do so."

Myra leaned in. "Now I just have to get *my* brood married off. Helena is far too content with her philanthropy work, and Louise keeps turning down eligible young men like she's selecting chocolates at a confectioner."

"They have good heads on their shoulders. You should be proud of them both."

"Oh, I am," Myra sighed dramatically. "But wouldn't it be lovely to marry one of them to someone with a title? A viscount, perhaps. Or an earl. Something impressive. Something European."

"The last thing I want is for Caroline to marry a peer of the realm."

Myra gasped. "Laura!"

"I mean it," Laura said, her tone light but firm. "I've read that half of them are bankrupt and looking for a rich American to fix the roof on their ancestral manor."

"Well, yes," Myra said, fanning faster. "But the romance of it!"

"I want Caroline to marry someone kind. Someone who values her spirit, not her dowry."

"Hmph." Myra gave her a sideways glance. "You're always so sensible."

Laura smiled faintly. "It's served me well."

Across the garden, Bert and Zella joined hands for the first waltz as husband and wife. Applause broke out as the couple turned, beaming, hand in hand.

Zella's gown—a soft champagne silk trimmed with antique lace—shimmered as she danced. Bert leaned in to murmur something to her, and she laughed in that delighted way Laura had come to recognize.

The reception unfolded with champagne toasts, strawberry shortcake, and dancing beneath paper lanterns. Charles gave a rare speech, touching briefly on Bert's childhood tendency to organize coin collections and correct his mother's household ledgers. There was laughter, and a moment of mistiness when Zella, unsentimental though she was, dabbed at her eyes.

Later, Laura stepped away from the crowd, needing a breath of quiet. She found it near the hydrangea hedge at the far end of the garden, where the air smelled of sun-warmed leaves and the music drifted like a memory.

Bert found her there a few minutes later.

"You're not hiding, are you?" he asked gently.

"Just resting," she said. "Your father will need rescuing from your grandmother soon."

He grinned. "I'll have Zella cajole him into a dance."

Laura turned to him, letting her eyes linger on his face. He looked more like his father every year, though the tenderness was all his own. "She's good for you," she said.

"She's everything," he answered.

Laura's throat tightened. She nodded and reached up to adjust the flower in his lapel. "Then don't let the world pull you apart. Not work, not pride."

"I know," he said softly. "We'll figure it out."

"On your terms," she said, echoing something she'd heard him tell Zella once.

He kissed her cheek and returned to the party, leaving Laura with the fading sun and her thoughts.

Behind her, Myra appeared, holding a small plate of cakes.

"I snuck two lemon tartlets," she whispered conspiratorially. "Don't tell James."

Laura laughed and took one. "Never."

They stood in silence a moment, watching the newlyweds dance beneath the lanterns.

"Maybe you're right," Myra said at last.

"About what?"

"About wanting our children to marry for love. Though if a marquess shows up from London asking after Alexandra, I won't turn him away."

Laura raised a brow. "You might have better luck with Max and the aristocratic set. He seems the type to charm his way through European drawing rooms."

"Him?" Myra huffed. "He'd marry a seamstress with a tragic past and call it destiny."

Laura smiled, savoring the tart sweetness on her tongue. "Well, at least it wouldn't be boring."

The band struck up another tune. Somewhere, Zella's laugh rang out, joined by Bert's quieter one.

Laura lifted her face to the stars just beginning to blink to life. Two of her sons had married for love. The good Lord had seen to that.

What more could a mother want?

Coming February 2026

Summoned to England by a grandmother she's never met, Helena "Lena" Dennison is determined to stay only a short time before returning to Philadelphia. She certainly didn't intend to meet a dashing barrister with a dangerous hobby—or to find herself intrigued despite her better judgment.

Bron Jeffers, known for his charm in court and his daring exploits behind the wheel of a motorcar, never expected to feel a strong attraction to a serious-minded American who refuses to be impressed. But when sabotage and danger strike close to home, Lena and Bron join forces—and discover that risking their hearts could be the most perilous gamble of all.

ALSO BY KIMBERLY KEAGAN

Perfect, Hearts on Display Book One
All Along, A Sweet Gilded Age Novelette

Heart of Hope (Hearts of the West, #15)

You can find links to Kimberly's books all in one place at: books2read.com/KimberlyKeagan.

Thank you for reading Bert and Zella's story. Your support means the world to me! If you enjoyed the book—and I hope you did—please take a quick minute to leave a review. It doesn't have to be long—just a sentence or two telling what you liked about the story.

This book wouldn't exist without the support of so many wonderful people. I'm especially grateful to my family and friends—your love and support keep me going; to my talented editors, Lynne Pearson and Sarah Smith; and to my incredible critique partners. Most of all, I give thanks and glory to my Lord and Savior, Jesus Christ.

Let's stay in touch, lovely reader! A great place to connect is through my *Puddings & Pages* email newsletter. As a thank-you, new subscribers receive a complimentary e-book. You can sign up at KimberlyKeagan.com or use the QR code below.

About the Author

Kimberly Keagan's love of romance novels started at the age of thirteen. Whenever she could get away with it, she ignored her chores in favor of a story she couldn't put down.

By God's grace, she married her own handsome hero, and together they raised two wonderful children. She earned a degree in accounting and enjoyed a career in investor relations, writing financial reports and press releases. Terrific jobs, but not very romantic.

Now, she's following her dream of writing her own historical romance stories with strong heroines, swoon-worthy heroes, and quirky secondary characters.

When not reading or writing, Kimberly likes to bake, garden, watch sports, and research her family tree.

Connect with Kimberly at: www.kimberlykeagan.com